"You have to know you're beautiful, Madison...."

Without meaning to, she touched her left cheek, fingering the scar there. He grabbed her hand and pulled it away.

"The scar doesn't matter," he said.

In that moment she believed him.

Quiet settled between them. She found herself getting lost in his dark eyes, searching them for emotions and secrets. Tanner cared. It took a while to uncover the feelings, but they were there.

She suddenly realized he still held her hand. Somehow his fingers were tangled in hers and it felt...right.

Why was she attracted to Tanner? Was it the situation—a victim wildly grateful to her rescuer? Was it that everything was so raw between them, so there wasn't time or energy for games? Was it the man himself?

Did it m

Dear Reader,

I don't know about you, but September makes me miss buying pencils and notebooks for school. Under cover of night (the only way for an Intimate Moments gal to go), I'll creep into a drugstore and buy the most garish notebook I can find, along with colored markers and neon erasers. Because you deserve to be pampered, why not treat yourself to September's fabulous batch of Silhouette Intimate Moments books, and at the same time maybe buy yourself some school supplies, too?

USA TODAY bestselling author Susan Mallery delights us with *Living on the Edge* (#1383), a sexy romance in which a rugged bodyguard rescues a feisty heiress from her abusive ex-husband. While cooped up in close quarters, these two strangers find they have sizzling chemistry. In *Perfect Assassin* (#1384), Wendy Rosnau captivates readers with the story of a dangerous woman who has learned how to take out a target. And she means to kill those who hurt her father. What happens when the target is the man she loves?

Hard Case Cowboy (#1385) by Nina Bruhns is a page-turning adventure in which two opposites have to run a ranch together. Can they deal with the hardships of ranch life and keep from falling head over heels in love? And in Diane Pershing's *Whispers and Lies* (#1386), an ugly-duckling-turned-swan stumbles upon her schoolgirl crush, who, unbeknownst to her, is investigating the scandalous secrets of her family. Their new relationship could be the biggest mistake ever…or a dream come true.

I wish you a happy September and hope you'll return next month to Intimate Moments, where your thirst for suspense and romance is sure to be satisfied. Happy reading!

Sincerely,

Patience Smith
Associate Senior Editor

Please address questions and book requests to:
Silhouette Reader Service
U.S.: 3010 Walden Ave., P.O. Box 1325, Buffalo, NY 14269
Canadian: P.O. Box 609, Fort Erie, Ont. L2A 5X3

SUSAN MALLERY

LIVING ON
THE EDGE

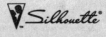

INTIMATE MOMENTS™

Published by Silhouette Books

America's Publisher of Contemporary Romance

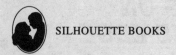 **SILHOUETTE BOOKS**

ISBN 0-373-27453-X

LIVING ON THE EDGE

Books by Susan Mallery

SUSAN MALLERY

is the bestselling and award-winning author of over fifty books for Harlequin and Silhouette Books. She makes her home in the Los Angeles area with her handsome prince of a husband and her two adorable-but-not-bright cats. Feel free to contact her via her Web site at www.susanmallery.com.

Chapter 1

Given the choice, Tanner Keane preferred darkness to light, and tonight was no exception. It had taken him forty-eight hours to find the woman and her kidnappers, but he'd waited another thirty-six before going to rescue her—just so he could learn about their schedule and then go in at night.

He liked the shadows, the silence, the fact that most people were asleep. Even those awake were on the low end of their energy cycle—although not his men. He made sure of that.

Tanner checked the time, then glanced back at the two-story house. After nearly two weeks of watching over the woman, the guards had grown sloppy and complacent. They patrolled the estate on a schedule now, instead of at random intervals. After so many days of quiet, they no longer expected trouble. All the better for him.

He reached for his night-vision binoculars and trained them on the second-story bedroom windows. The third one from the left had open drapes, which allowed him a view of the darkened room. A woman paced there—restless, worried, scared.

Tall and willowy, she moved with the grace of someone trained in dance…and the lifestyles of the rich and famous. Blond, beautiful and worth about five hundred million—if he counted her daddy's share of the family's net worth.

Oh, yeah, he knew pretty much everything about her and he wasn't impressed. Even now, he didn't shift his binoculars to *her*. She was the target, but incidental to the moment. What he really needed to know was who else was in the room with her. How many watchers had been left on duty?

There were a total of five assigned to her—usually working in shifts of two. Except at night. From midnight until seven, there was only one woman keeping watch.

He scanned the room and saw the guard sitting in a chair in the corner of the room. From the tilt of her head, he would guess she'd fallen asleep.

Sloppy, he thought. If she worked for him, she would be fired. But she didn't, and her bad habits were his gain.

He turned his attention back to the prisoner. Madison Hilliard crossed to the French doors and opened them. After glancing over her shoulder to make sure her keeper continued to doze, she stepped out into the cool California night and walked to the railing.

Her life had taken a turn for the unpleasant, Tanner thought without sympathy. Two weeks ago she'd been living in her rich-woman world and now she was held captive, threatened and never left alone. That was enough to ruin anyone's day.

"Red Two, go," a voice murmured into Tanner's earpiece.

Tanner tapped the tiny device by way of a response. He was the operative closest to the mansion. Until it was time, he wouldn't be doing any talking.

Madison lingered by the railing. Tanner tucked his binoculars in his backpack. There was no point in looking at her—he'd spent the past four days studying everything about her. He knew her age, her marital status, distinguishing marks, where she liked to shop and how very little she did with her day. She might be worth enough to keep a man in style, but she wasn't his type. Not her pedigree, not her life, not her body. Rich women tended to be high maintenance, and Tanner liked his women easy…very easy.

He checked his watch again. Nearly time. He tapped once on his earpiece, then reached for his gun.

The modified pistol in his hand shot strong, incredibly fast sedatives. They incapacitated in less than five seconds. He preferred something a little faster, but this operation required more finesse than usual, and he couldn't risk the potentially fatal reaction to a quicker-acting chemical. The client had insisted on no dead bodies.

Pity, Tanner thought as he began to creep toward the glass doors on the side of the house. He didn't have much sympathy or patience for kidnappers. The outra-

geous ransom—twenty million dollars worth of un-
marked bills in multiple foreign denominations—had
annoyed him. He hated when criminals watched too
much TV and took their ideas from bad spy movies. To
his mind they should either act like pros or stay out of
the game.

He reached the glass doors and waited. In less than
three minutes, two things occurred simultaneously.
Brody, their alarm maestro, tapped the "all clear" sig-
nal on his earpiece. A quick double click told Tanner
that the system was down. Brody was good enough to
keep the cameras moving back and forth while all the
red lights continued blinking just as they should. The
only difference was the alarm wouldn't go off.

The second thing that happened was a guard strolled
by, right on time.

Dumb-ass, Tanner thought as he spun silently,
popped the guy full of sedative and held him immobile
for five seconds. He dropped the dead weight not too
gently onto the patio and rolled him out of sight next to
the planter. There wasn't any sound.

He touched his earpiece twice. Three more individual clicks followed.

"Red Two, go," a soft voice came again.

Angel, Tanner's best sniper, sat up high in a tree, out
of range of the action. He kept an eye on everything happening. Only an idiot walked into hell without an angel
watching for trouble.

Tanner moved to the locked glass doors and removed
a small container from his utility belt. One minute later,
the custom acid mixture turned the locking mechanism

to mush and he was in. He pulled on night-vision goggles, double-clicked his earpiece to tell the team he'd completed the next phase of the operation and headed for the stairs.

At the top of the landing he encountered and immobilized another guard. But he didn't head to the door midway down the hallway. Not until he'd heard three more individual clicks, followed by a soft "Red Two, go."

Still clear.

Tanner emptied his mind of everything unessential. The floor plan of the suite had been etched into his brain. When last he'd seen Madison, she'd been on the balcony. Given her few freedoms in the past couple of weeks, he doubted she would have moved. Her guard would still be sleeping on the job. One shot would take care of her. With a little luck, she wouldn't know what hit her.

He turned the container he still held and shot the second blast of acid from the back end. A slow count to sixty, then he eased the door open.

"Man on the stairs, Tanner. Watch your back."

Tanner swore under his breath. There was an extra man on duty tonight. Wasn't that always the way?

He left the door, pivoted and pressed his body into the shadows. Someone walked into view, his gun drawn.

"Natalie, are you all right? There's been some trouble. A.J.'s missing."

"What?"

When things went to hell, they did so at light speed. Madison's female guard—aka Natalie—stumbled from her seat. Tanner heard the sound just as he zapped the

guard. Unfortunately she tried the door and found it un-
locked. There was the sound of a pistol being cocked.

Tanner dropped the guard onto the landing and
waited for Natalie to come out, hoping she was just stupid enough not to follow orders. That rather than staying with her prisoner, she would venture onto the
landing.

Sure enough, the door cracked open. He got her in
the arm before she cleared the threshold. Which left
Madison Hilliard all alone.

Tanner dragged a now-unconscious Natalie out of
the way and headed into the suite. He hoped he didn't
have to go looking for the rich princess. He also hoped
she wasn't a screamer. He hated screamers…well, not
in bed.

But Madison hadn't hidden. She still stood by the
railing, watching him approach.

"I'm one of the good guys," he said. "Let's move."

Her long hair hid most of her face, but he thought he
saw her smile. Coolly, though. Not with relief. She
wasn't going to throw herself at him with gratitude, but
at least she didn't seem to be a screamer.

"I always thought my rescuer would have a better
line than that. Maybe 'Come with me if you want to
live.'"

Tanner couldn't help an answering grin. "Yeah, I'm
a *Terminator* fan, too, but I'd rather talk on the helicopter. Unless you'd like to stay here?"

She didn't answer. Instead she walked toward him.

"Shoes," he said. "Don't sweat which ones. We're not
going to a fashion show."

She stuffed her feet into loafers and hurried toward the door. He followed her. Once they reached the landing, he took the lead. After grabbing her hand in his, he hustled them down the stairs.

There was no point in telling the team he had her; everyone would have heard their conversation.

"You're clear," Angel said quietly. "Chopper will be here in thirty."

They headed out the rear of the house. Tanner pulled off the night-vision goggles as they went. The rumble of a helicopter started in the distance while he and Madison hovered by the edge of the patio.

"How did you find me?" she asked.

He glanced at her. "That's my job."

"Ah. The strong, silent type. That must have impressed my father."

Tanner looked at her for the first time. Really looked. Madison Hilliard was no longer a glossy photo, but a real, breathing woman. Her long blond hair began to fly around her face as the helicopter started to descend. She tried to hold it at the back of her neck. One of the lights from the copter caught her full in the face.

Not much shocked Tanner—not anymore. But he was unprepared for the ugly slash scarring her left cheek and the way it contrasted with the beauty of her face. She saw him watching—staring—but didn't blink or turn away.

The helicopter landed. Before they could board, there was a yell from behind the house. Tanner swore and turned in that direction.

"Two guards," Angel said into his earpiece. "Son of

a bitch. Early shift change. They just drove up. Kelly, get down. On your left. On your—"

The sound of gunfire cut out the rest of Angel's words. The pitch and volume of the blasts told Tanner they hadn't all come from his men's guns. Not good, he thought grimly. His team quietly checked in, except for Kelly.

"Go," he told the woman, pushing her into the helicopter.

Madison scrambled inside.

Tanner hated stepping in next to her, but his men were trained. They would fan out and find their fallen team member. Sure enough, less than two minutes later, three men appeared, although only two were walking. They carried the third between them.

"Get going," Angel said into Tanner's earpiece. "Kelly got both of the other men after they got him, but they'd already made a call requesting backup."

"Will do. You get out of there, as well."

"I'm already gone, boss."

Tanner helped his men drag an unconscious and bleeding Kelly onto the floor of the helicopter, then he signaled for the pilot to take them up.

As they rose high in the sky, he checked his man. Two gunshots, both bad. One in the chest, one in the leg. Dammit all to hell, he thought grimly and glared at the woman huddled in the far seat. There were things worth dying for, but saving someone like her wasn't one of them.

The other two team members had already started emergency first aid. Tanner moved back to give them room. He picked up a headset and motioned for Madison to do the same.

"Your reunion is going to have to wait," he told her, speaking into the attached microphone. "I need to get my man to a doctor."

Her gaze moved from him to Kelly, then back. "Of course. I can stay with you at the hospital."

There was no point in telling her they weren't going to a hospital. Public health facilities required too much paperwork, and the staff would have too many questions. Tanner had his own state-of-the-art medical center with trained specialists—all former military doctors—on call.

"One of my men will take you to a safe place," Tanner told her. "You can wait there until I'm available to return you to your family."

He figured Madison and her husband could hold on an extra hour or two before seeing each other. As his was the only face his clients ever saw, he would have to return her himself. Just as well—he could pick up his sizable check at the same time.

He jerked off the headset and fought his temper. It should have been an easy job, he told himself. No one was supposed to get hurt. Certainly not Kelly—the youngest and newest member of their team. Kelly had just gotten engaged the previous month. He was from Iowa, for God's sake. This wasn't supposed to happen to a kid from Iowa.

Madison Hilliard paced the length and width of the small room. She had no idea how long she'd been held there—no windows provided light, she wasn't wearing a watch and she couldn't find a clock. She figured at least a couple of hours had passed. Maybe more.

The space was spare to the point of being monastic—
a single bed, a sink and a toilet. No closet, no desk.
Nothing to read, nothing to look at, nothing to do. She
supposed she should have slept—she hadn't been able
to do more than doze since the kidnapping. But anxiety
kept her moving. While she wanted to believe she'd
been rescued, she knew it was unlikely.

Fear gripped her. In the past twelve days she'd grown
used to the cold fingers clutching her midsection and the
sense of looming disaster. She tried to tell herself that
someone, somewhere would miss her. That her clients
would ask questions, that her friends would notice she'd
disappeared. But would they? Wouldn't Christopher have
already thought of that and planned for the contingency?

The only door in the room was locked from the outside. She'd already tried it several times. There was no
way she could break through the metal door and she
doubted she could claw through the walls. So she was
trapped until her rescuer returned to reunite her with her
family. And then?

How long would Christopher keep her alive? A few
weeks? Months? She didn't know his plan, so she wasn't
sure if he needed her. That need was her only hope.

A faint sound came from the hallway. Madison
turned and braced herself for the inevitable. For the
sight of the man who wanted her dead. Instead the door
opened and her rescuer stood in front of her.

He was tall, muscular and dark in a way that went
deeper than his black hair and brown eyes. He was the
kind of man people walked around rather than con-
fronted. Power and confidence surrounded him like a

visible aura. He wore black and there was a gun at his belt. How much did he know? Would he be using the gun on her?

"Sorry to have kept you waiting," the man said, sounding more angry than actually sorry.

"It's all right. How is your friend?"

"Still in surgery."

"I hope he's going to be all right." She didn't need the weight of a stranger's injuries on her already burdened conscience.

A case could be made that the shooting wasn't her fault—she hadn't asked to be rescued or even kidnapped in the first place. But the injured man had been there because of her, and she couldn't make herself believe she wasn't somehow responsible.

The man in front of her looked her over. "Are you hungry? Did they feed you?"

"I'm fine." She couldn't imagine ever eating again. She couldn't imagine life ever being normal. "I'm sorry, I didn't get your name."

"Keane. Tanner Keane."

"Mr. Keane, I'm assuming my family hired you to find me?"

He nodded and crossed his arms over his chest. "Call me Tanner. And yes, your husband and your father came to me a few days ago. They'd hired another company to locate you after the kidnapping, but they didn't have much luck." He raised one shoulder, then let it fall. "I'm better."

Interesting. Why would Christopher have gone to someone who wasn't the best? He hated dealing with anyone who wasn't completely qualified. She tried to focus on the question, on the point of it all, but lack of sleep made her fuzzy.

It had to be about money, she told herself. But how?

"Was there a ransom?" she asked.

"Twenty million."

Madison felt her head start to swim. "That much." She crossed to the bed and sank down onto the mattress. "Was it paid?"

"It would have been." Tanner glanced at his watch. "In about two hours. I put in a call to have it intercepted. I'll be returning the money to your family when I take you to them."

Which was the problem, she thought. "My father hired you?"

"And your husband. They're both very anxious to get you back. It's understandable. This has been difficult for them, as well."

Madison fought the urge to laugh. She had a feeling any humor would quickly explode into hysterics. Once she lost control, she might never get it back.

"Mr. Keane—Tanner—I don't want to be returned to my family."

One dark eyebrow rose slowly. "Why is that?"

"Do you need a reason? Can't you simply let me go?"

"My contract with your family states that I return you to them. I would have done it right away, but Kelly's medical treatment took priority."

"I know and it's fine. I just…" She stared at him, wondering how to make this man understand. "Unless you're planning to hold me captive, as well, I should be free to go."

If only he would agree. She could easily disappear—Los Angeles was a huge place and she had friends no one knew about.

"I can't have you wandering the streets with no money or identification."

Oh, right. No credit cards, either, although she didn't think she could use them. Christopher would be able to track her.

Tanner gave her a smile that didn't come close to reaching his eyes. "Mrs. Hilliard, you've been through a very traumatic experience. You're confused, and that's understandable. I'm sure when you're back home with your husband and your father, you'll feel much better. In a few weeks, you'll be able to put this whole experience behind you."

"I hope you're right. Unfortunately I think there's also a very good chance I'll be dead."

Chapter 2

Tanner held in a groan. He had neither the time nor the patience to deal with a drama queen right now. He wanted Madison Hilliard out of his life so he could focus on what was important. Dammit all to hell, what was it about rich women and their need to be the center of the universe?

"Wasn't the kidnapping enough for one week?" he asked, barely able to restrain his temper.

"I'm not playing a game," she said, her eyes wide with a lot of emotion he wasn't interested in reading. "You can't return me to my family. Take me anywhere else. Please."

"How about a police station?"

She considered that option. Funny how he wasn't surprised when she slowly shook her head. The cops wouldn't be the kind of audience that interested her. They wouldn't be willing to play her little game, either.

He narrowed his gaze as he wondered if mental problems ran in her family.

She took a step toward him. "Christopher is the one who kidnapped me. I was attacked and drugged as I walked into my condo. I couldn't see anyone, but I recognized his watch right before I passed out. It's very distinctive—he had it custom-made."

"Uh-huh." He would have to give her points for originality, if nothing else. "Can you prove it?"

"What? Of course not. It was a kidnapping. It's not as if they sent me an itinerary ahead of time and used Christopher's letterhead. But I know what I saw."

Sure. "So tell me, Madison, why would your husband want to kidnap you?"

"I don't know. I guess he needed the money."

"You both already have plenty of that."

"Christopher doesn't have as much as you'd think. He's always running short of cash. That's the only thing that explains the excessive ransom."

"Twenty million is a hell of a lot for him to need."

She nodded. "Please. I know how this sounds. I know you have no reason to trust me, but things are not as they seem. Christopher lives on the edge. He gambles and usually loses a lot. He buys expensive pieces of art and furniture. Trust me, he always needs more money."

"Nothing personal, Mrs. Hilliard, but I *don't* trust you."

"You don't like me, either," Madison said. "That's okay. But it doesn't give you the right to put me at risk."

"I don't believe you are. Why would your husband

have hired two different companies to find you if he wanted you dead?"

"Because I'm worth more to him alive. You don't actually know he hired another company. He could be lying."

"Sure, and so could you." Tanner reached the end of his attention span for this conversation. "I was hired by your husband and your father to find you, and I did. Because of that, one of my best men is close to death. All I want is my fee and you out of my life. I'm not interested in getting involved in whatever sick game you and your husband are playing."

With that, he turned and headed for the door.

Madison rushed toward him. "We're not married. Did he tell you that? We've been divorced for over six months. I'm sure there's a way you could check the court records to verify it."

Tanner stared at her. Divorced? He glanced at her left hand. No ring and no marks to show one had been removed recently. Neither Hilliard nor her father had said anything about a divorce. In fact, Hilliard had made it very clear he wanted his wife home with him, where she belonged. Tanner remembered wondering about Mrs. Hilliard's feelings on being such an important possession.

Not that it changed anything, he told himself. Divorced or not, he'd been paid to complete a job and he had. Except…

He swore under his breath. There was something about her desperation, something about her words and, most important, something about the tension in his gut. He'd learned from hard experience to never ignore that feeling.

Madison must have sensed she had his attention, because she started talking very quickly.

"I left him nearly two years ago. He spent the first six months trying to convince me to come back and the next year fighting the divorce. Fortunately California is a no-fault state, and in the end, he couldn't stop it."

"Why was he so interested in keeping a woman who wanted to get away?"

"Money."

"You've brought that up before. Your ex is loaded."

She shook her head. "No. He's not. His lifestyle sucks up a lot of his company profits. Plus he's into something big. I don't know what it is—I've only heard my father talking about it from time to time."

"Didn't he get a big chunk of your net worth after the divorce?"

"No. There was a pretty tight prenuptial agreement." For the first time since he'd met her, she smiled. "Besides, I'm not worth all that much on my own. The bulk of the family fortune is tied up in Adams Electronics. My father is the principal stockholder, not me. I only own a few thousand shares. Christopher did get the house, which was fine with me."

So Hilliard had lost the eye-candy wife *and* access to the big bucks. That couldn't have made him happy.

"He and your father are working on something together. It came up in my research," Tanner told her.

"I know. I've read the same thing. I don't talk to my father about it. I've tried to convince him to stop doing business with Christopher, but he won't listen. He doesn't understand how I could have let such a good man get away."

She tilted her head, which caused her long blond hair to fall away from her face, exposing the side with the still-red scar. He narrowed his gaze. Why would such a beautiful woman keep such an ugly mark on her face? She would have had access to the best plastic surgeons in the world, along with the money to pay them. As much as he hated to admit it, a lot of things didn't make sense.

"He set up the kidnapping to get the ransom money," she said earnestly. "I doubt there was any other company looking for me. I'm sure he told my father there was to keep him from worrying."

"Why wouldn't your father have insisted on going to the police?"

Her mouth twisted. "He trusts Christopher implicitly. As far as he was concerned, his son-in-law would handle everything perfectly." She glanced down at the floor, then back at him. "My father is something of an absent-minded professor. He likes it best when the real world doesn't interfere with his time in the lab."

Which meant what? That her father hadn't been all that worried about the kidnapping because good old Hilliard was taking care of it?

Tanner recalled his meeting with the two men. Hilliard had done all the talking. Blaine Adams had seemed concerned, but not overly so.

"If nothing else, you should make sure you get paid," Madison told him. "My ex has a bad habit of offering fees in halves. Half up front, half at the end of the deal. Only that second half doesn't ever seem to get paid."

"Hilliard wouldn't try that with me."

"How do you know?"

"Because I'd hunt him down and make him beg to give me the rest of my money."

"Good luck with that."

She spoke with the confidence of someone who had lived the truth. Tanner grimaced as he realized he'd carefully checked out Blaine Adams when he'd taken the job, but he'd only done a cursory check on Hilliard. After all, Daddy had been the one paying the ransom. But Hilliard had offered to take care of the bill.

Sloppy work, he told himself. Sloppy gets you dead.

He glared at Madison. He didn't have time for this or her or her sob story. He wanted her gone. But he couldn't—not with his gut whispering that she just might be telling the truth. Hilliard kidnapping his ex-wife to get his hands on the family money wasn't his business, but he wouldn't send her back if she was at risk. No matter how much he wanted to.

He was going to have to check out her story.

"I don't believe you for a second," he said flatly. "But I'll look into what you've told me."

Her relief was a tangible creature in the room. Before she could get too relaxed, Tanner moved close and cupped her neck. He applied just enough pressure to make it difficult for her to breathe.

"If you're playing me for a fool, I'll make you sorry. Is that clear?"

Her eyes widened. Color fled her face, but her gaze never wavered. She stared right back at him and slowly nodded.

He acknowledged that she hadn't flinched. At least she had some backbone. And she wasn't a screamer. Two small points in her favor.

When he released her, she stood her ground. She didn't whimper or complain or even rub her neck.

"You don't understand," she told him quietly. "There's nothing you can do that's worse than what Christopher has already done to me. I'm not trying to trick you, I just want to stay alive."

Funny how at that moment, he almost wanted it to be true. That she was just what she said.

Not a snowball's chance, he thought. He studied her face, her long blond hair, her slender body. Except for the scar, she was perfect. Tall, leggy, beautiful. And completely useless.

He had no time for women like her in his life, but he wouldn't mind finding her in his bed—just for the night. She would be a hell of a ride.

Tanner left Madison in the holding cell and returned to the front office of the small warehouse building he rented down by the airport. His laptop sprang to life when he hit the keys. Seconds later, he was on the Internet and tapping into sources to check out what Madison had said about her ex.

Two hours later, he had a detailed financial profile of Christopher Hilliard, along with e-mails from two informants. Word on the street *was* that Hilliard had a habit of skipping out on bills. An interesting practice for someone born to money. There were also some hints about shady dealings, but nothing specific. The most interesting point came from a casino employee Tanner had on retainer. Hilliard liked the high-stakes games, but they didn't like him. He was up to his eyeballs in serious debt to some not-friendly people. Could that be why he needed the ransom money?

Speaking of which… He made a quick call, then leaned back in his chair. Now what? While he didn't want to believe Madison, so far he hadn't caught her in a lie. Sure, she wasn't anyone he could respect, but that didn't mean he wanted her dead. And until he was sure, she remained his responsibility.

Might as well get it over with, he told himself as he reached for the phone again. This time he called Blaine Adams's house. The older man picked up on the first ring.

"Adams here."

"Tanner Keane."

"At last. Hold on, Mr. Keane." There was a second of silence followed by Adams saying, "Christopher, it's Mr. Keane. Pick up in the library."

Tanner waited through the quiet. Then he heard a click and Hilliard was on the line.

"Keane? What the hell is going on? Where's my wife?"

Ex-wife, Tanner thought, wondering who was playing what game with him.

"I have her with me. She's safe."

Blaine breathed a sigh of relief. "Thank God. I should have listened to you before, Christopher. You said Mr. Keane was the best. Is Madison all right?"

"She's perfectly fine. Anxious to see you both."

"Good, good. Well done." Blaine cleared his throat.

"All right, then. Christopher, I'll leave this to you. I need to get back to the lab. I have a meeting, some work…"

His voice trailed off as if he'd already left but had forgotten to hang up the phone. Seconds later, the receiver had been replaced.

Tanner had tried to think of ways to get Blaine off the phone, but it turned out fate had been kind. Now it was just him and Hilliard.

"You must have been worried," Tanner said.

"Of course. We've all been sick. That other company I hired—what a bunch of incompetent asses."

"I'm sorry you had to go through that." Tanner leaned back in his chair and prepared to begin the game. "What was the name of the company? The first one you hired."

"Why do you want to know?"

"People ask me about the competition. I don't want to recommend someone who can't do the job."

Hilliard chuckled. "I doubt you recommend anyone, Keane."

Interesting. So Hilliard wasn't going to tell him. Which made Tanner wonder if Madison had been right—maybe there *hadn't* been a first company. Maybe Hilliard had simply waited to hire Tanner to make things look more desperate. That would help Blaine come to terms with such a steep ransom.

"How is she? Really, I mean," Hilliard said. "Madison was never very strong emotionally."

"Relieved. They beat her up pretty badly."

"What? No. They wouldn't have."

Tanner nodded slowly. Not exactly the normal response of a worried and grieving husband.

"Why would they do that?" Hilliard ask. "They wanted ransom money, not to hurt her. I didn't think kidnappers hurt their victims. I want those people found. I want them punished for what they did to my wife."

It wasn't much of a recovery, Tanner thought, but then maybe he was reading too much into the conversation. Still, it was interesting that Hilliard characterized his wife as emotionally weak. From what Tanner had seen of Madison, she was tough. She'd been through hell, possibly at the hands of her ex-husband, and she was still holding it together.

"Not my line of work," Tanner told him. "You'll have to find someone else for that job. Oh, I almost forgot. About the ransom…" He paused deliberately, giving Hilliard time to sweat.

"Yes? It was paid."

"No. Once I had Madison, I sent my men to intercept it."

There was only silence. Tanner waited. If Hilliard wasn't involved and if he hadn't done it for the money, he wouldn't care one way or the other.

"Where is the money now?" Hilliard asked, his voice carefully neutral.

But Tanner had been in the business for too long to be fooled. The other man was angry and frustrated. He'd wanted the ransom delivered. Dammit all to hell, he thought grimly. Madison was right. Her ex was in this up to his eyeballs. But how? And why?

Questions to be answered later.

"I'm having the ransom delivered to Mr. Adams at his office. I've notified his banker, as well, so he'll be there to take possession of the money. It's a lot of cash to have lying around. I wouldn't want anything to happen to it."

"You're very thorough," Hilliard said, his rage barely concealed.

"That's what you pay me to be. Speaking of which, you owe me the second half of my fee."

"Yes. Of course." Hilliard sucked in a breath. "Where is Madison? Are you having her delivered to her father's office, as well?"

"That's a funny thing," Tanner said, enjoying the moment. "She's pretty shaken, as you can imagine. Right now she just wants to lay low for a while."

"What, exactly, does that mean?"

"She'll be my guest for a few days."

Hilliard swore. "You can't do that. You're just as bad as they are. I suppose we'll be getting a ransom demand from you, as well."

"I'm not holding your wife against her will, Mr. Hilliard. This is at her very specific request."

"I want my wife back immediately. It's what you were hired to do. If you don't return her, I'll go to the police."

"In your position, that's what I'd do, as well," Tanner told him.

"You can't do this."

"I just did."

Tanner hung up the phone and wondered what would happen next. If he and Madison were wrong and Hilliard wasn't playing a game, he would go directly to the police. But Tanner doubted that was likely. There was something going on—something that had cost Hilliard twenty million dollars.

Christopher did his best to lose himself in work, but it was impossible. Rage interfered with his concentration. How could things have gone so badly?

He knew Madison was responsible. The bitch had been nothing but an impediment for the past three years. He'd married her expecting someone beautiful and brainless to decorate his world. Instead she'd gotten a job, gotten involved and made his life a living hell. She had opinions, damn her.

His phone rang. He wanted to rip it out of the wall, but he forced himself to answer it.

"Hilliard," he said.

"Ah, Christopher. So glad I caught you." Blaine Adams rambled on about problems with a circuit board.

Christopher tried to concentrate and offer reasonable suggestions when what he really wanted was to ask the old man how he could be so stupid. Didn't he realize what was going on in his own company or with his own daughter? Better for Christopher that he didn't, but how could one person be so unaware?

"Oh," the older man said when they'd finished the mini brainstorming session. "A very nice young man stopped by earlier with the ransom money. That Mr. Keane said it would be delivered here, and it was. My banker has already taken possession of it. You were right to hire that Mr. Keane. A fine man."

"One of the best," Christopher said between clenched teeth. "I'd heard Keane was efficient."

"And so he was. Now Madison can concentrate on relaxing and getting over this horrible ordeal. You'll be there for her, won't you, Christopher?"

"Of course. You know Madison is my life."

"Yes, yes. It's a pity she got so headstrong and left. I'm sure it was nothing but a misunderstanding. I'm counting on you to win her back. Show her your soft side. She'll need that over the next few weeks. Unfortunately my little girl has too much of her mother in her. Little can be done with a weak mind."

"I love her anyway," Christopher said.

"I know. You're a good man. Like a son to me." Blaine chuckled. "What a cliché. All right, back to work, my boy. The same for me. These problems won't solve themselves, will they?"

With that, the old man hung up. Christopher slammed the receiver back into place. What he wouldn't give to get his hands on Madison. He wouldn't just show her his softer side, as her father had requested, he would strangle the bitch with his bare hands.

How had it all gone wrong? Keane wasn't supposed to intercept the ransom. Christopher had been counting on that money. He'd needed fifteen of the twenty million for his next payment to Stanislav. The Russian Mafia did *not* like to be kept waiting. The remaining five million had been to cover his gambling losses. What the hell was he supposed to do now?

He stood, crossed to the credenza against the wall, picked up the vase there and threw it into the closed door. The loud smash followed by the rain of shards on the hardwood floor made him feel better for a brief second or two, but then desperation and panic returned.

He needed the next phase of the jamming system. He'd already arranged a press conference to announce it and if he canceled now, people would talk. Word would travel around the industry that his program was in trouble. No, he had to get the money somehow.

He returned to his desk and glanced at the calendar. There wasn't much time left. Stanislav had warned him that if he was late again, the Russian would find another buyer. Christopher couldn't let that happen. He needed the cutting-edge technology and the billions it would bring in to his company and, therefore, to him. He wanted to be the biggest and the best, then he wanted to destroy everyone who had ever said he couldn't do it.

And he wanted Madison back. He wanted her crawling, broken and bleeding. He would use her until she begged and then he would kill her.

When that happened, it would be a very good day.

Chapter 3

Madison walked back and forth in the small room until her legs and back ached, then she perched on the edge of the bed and stared at the door. Once again, she had no idea of how much time had passed or when Tanner Keane would return. She only knew she was desperately afraid he wouldn't find whatever he'd gone looking for and that he would return her to Christopher. One thing she'd learned in the past few days was that she wasn't ready to die.

She rested her elbows on her thighs and dropped her head to her hands. Thoughts swirled—a kaleidoscope of the mistakes she'd made that had brought her to this place. Had it started when she'd fallen for Christopher, or did the roots go deeper than that? Had her first sin been committed when she'd grown up spoiled and selfish, never looking at the world beyond what it could offer her?

A sound caught her attention. She straightened, then stood, only to sink back onto the bed when the room seemed to swim around her. In the time it took to clear her head, the door opened and Tanner stepped inside.

She forced herself to her feet and stared at him. His expression gave nothing away, which shouldn't surprise her. She wanted to speak, to ask about her fate, but her mouth was too dry. The ever-present fear grew until it pushed the air out of her body.

"I had an interesting talk with your husband," he said as he leaned against the door frame and crossed his arms over his chest.

"Ex-husband," she whispered, never taking her gaze from his face.

"Funny how he doesn't mention that, although I checked on the records, and you're right. The divorce is final."

Some small measure of relief battled for space with the fear. Did that mean he would believe her? That she could be safe for a little while longer?

She waited, instinctively knowing it would be better if *he* spoke rather than her.

"I don't believe you," he said flatly.

The blood seemed to rush from her body, leaving her cold and boneless. She sank to the bed as the room spun and a high-pitched sound filled her head.

"But I don't believe him, either."

Madison blinked. "W-what?"

"Something's not right. I think you're a rich bitch

drama queen, but I'm not convinced your ex is telling the truth. There are secrets on both sides, and I want to know what they are."

He defined her in words designed to wound, but right now she didn't care what he thought of her.

"You're not sending me back?" she asked, barely daring to hope.

"Not yet."

Fear receded, leaving little to support her, and she swayed slightly. Tanner frowned.

"When was the last time you ate or slept?" he asked.

"It's been a while."

His face tightened with contempt. "I know it's stylish to be stick-thin, but starvation isn't much of a fashion statement."

She shook her head. "It wasn't like that. I couldn't eat there. Or sleep. This isn't about being on a diet. I just…" She drew in a breath. "Have you ever been kidnapped? It's not a restful situation."

He didn't look convinced. The man didn't like her, and she found the realization oddly comforting. He didn't want anything from her except the truth. He was good enough not to be willing to return her to a situation that might be dangerous, but he wasn't interested in what he could get from her.

But she did have something to offer him.

"I'll pay you for your protection," she said. "Double whatever Christopher offered you."

Tanner's gaze narrowed and his mouth twisted. "Don't make me think less of you than I already do," he said flatly. "I'm not doing this for the money."

She wanted to ask why he was then. Why didn't he just let her go and be killed? But she didn't—there was no point in pushing him.

"I find it interesting that you've taken such a dislike to me when you don't know me at all," she said instead.

"I know your type."

"What type is that?"

"Rich. Useless."

He spoke with a certainty that told her she wasn't the first wealthy woman to cross his path and that whoever had done it before had scarred him in some way. A lover? A client?

Tanner straightened. "I'm moving you to a safe house. No one will be able to find you there, so you can eat and get some sleep. I'll keep on investigating Hilliard. If I turn up enough evidence to validate what you've told me, we'll talk about you hiring me to protect you. If you're lying…"

His voice trailed off. She had no doubt there would be some serious punishment involved. Still, she wondered if he could come up with anything worse than what she'd already endured. He didn't seem to be the type to use physical force against someone so ill equipped to handle it. She supposed rape was a possibility, but she doubted that was his style. Wasn't rape supposed to be about power? Tanner was the most powerful man she'd ever met. He would hardly need to prove himself.

Oh, but he would think of something. She was confident. She supposed she should worry about that, but she couldn't. After all she'd been through in the past ten days, she couldn't find the strength to be any more afraid.

"I accept your terms."

One corner of his mouth turned up in an almost smile. "You don't have a choice."

"Perhaps not, but I accept them anyway."

"I'm going to have to blindfold you. The safe house works only as long as no one knows where it is. If the idea of a blindfold freaks you out, I can sedate you."

The idea of a blindfold terrified her. It was too much like being kidnapped all over again. But the thought of being drugged was worse.

"I prefer the blindfold. I don't like the idea of losing control."

"Some people spend their whole lives looking for the perfect way to do just that."

"Not me." She stared at him and had the odd thought she very much wanted him to like her. "I'm not what you think."

He looked instantly bored. "I'll be right back."

He walked out of the room, leaving the door open. Madison stared at the narrow concrete hallway and wondered if his actions were a test to see if she could be trusted. It didn't matter. She had no plans to bolt for freedom. Right now Tanner was all that stood between her and Christopher. She already knew what her ex-husband was capable of. For now she was more than willing to put her fate into the hands of a stranger. With Tanner, the odds were a whole lot better.

If Madison had been asked to guess, she would have said the drive had taken about forty-five minutes. She'd been put in the rear of a van of some kind. There weren't any seats, but there were plenty of blankets. She'd curled up on them and listened to the sound of the engine and the road. Exhaustion had claimed her a few times and she'd dozed for a second or two.

When the van stopped, she straightened. She heard a garage door opening, then the van moved forward and the garage door closed behind it. There was the click of the lock followed by the creak of metal as the rear of the vehicle opened.

"You can take off the blindfold now," Tanner said.

For reasons that had made no sense to her, he hadn't tied her hands. She reached up and pulled off the blindfold, only to find herself in a dark box inside a van. Of course, she thought, knowing that if she'd been less exhausted she would have found the situation humorous. He hadn't tied her hands because once she was in the van it hadn't mattered if she'd removed the blindfold. There was nothing for her to see.

Very slick, she thought as she crawled to the end of the van and stepped down.

Lack of food and sleep made her shaky. She stumbled as she tried to stand. He grabbed her by the arm and held her steady.

"You've been tough all through this," he said gruffly. "Don't faint on me now."

"I won't," she promised, although she wasn't completely sure of her facts.

"Come on. I'll give you the quick tour, then you can crash for a few hours."

Sleep sounded like heaven. Maybe here, with Tanner watching over her, she would feel comfortable enough to relax.

He released her arm and motioned for her to step around him. After closing the back of the van, he led the way into the house.

She wasn't sure what she'd expected—perhaps some high-tech, modern space done in shades of white. What she found instead was a sprawling single-story ranch-style home with a few modifications.

From the garage they passed through a laundry room and into a hallway that led into a large family room. There was a big-screen television and several electronic components, along with two black leather sofas. The house itself might be forty or fifty years old, but the paint and the furniture looked relatively new.

Madison glanced at the ceiling, looking for cameras or some kind of monitoring device. She didn't see any. She did notice a strange screening material over the windows and pointed to it.

"No one can see in," Tanner said. "And you can't get out. But the windows all open if you feel the need for fresh air."

She was less worried about that than being trapped. "What if there's a fire?"

"There won't be."

He walked into a large kitchen and pointed out the basic amenities. There was already plenty of food in the refrigerator and pantry. Simple things that were easy to prepare.

"Help yourself," he told her.

She nodded, knowing she had to eat something eventually, but right now all she wanted was sleep.

Next up was what would have been the formal living and dining room. Instead she saw several desks and shelves, all crammed with electronic equipment. None of it made sense to her. There were screens and keyboards and odd display units.

Tanner stepped inside and grabbed something from a nearly empty desk. She didn't see what it was until he returned to her side and snapped it on her wrist.

"What on earth?" She stared at the gray metal bracelet. There was no visible catch, no markings of any kind.

"My game, my rules," he said. "You play by them or I return you to your ex."

"Why?" she asked, not sure if she was asking why he'd done it or why she didn't get a say in the rules.

"I don't trust you," he said flatly.

Good to know where she stood. "You could just let me go. I'll be fine on my own."

"If he's everything you say, he'll find you within twenty-four hours. Is that what you want?"

No, but she didn't want this either, she thought as she rubbed the bracelet. "What does it do?"

"Keeps you safe and keeps you here." He motioned to the control center of the house.

Madison glanced at him, then back to the bracelet before taking a step forward.

"You have entered an unauthorized area," a female computerized voice said. "Please return to an authorized area or an alarm will sound."

She jumped back. "It's some kind of monitoring system."

"Exactly. You can go anywhere you want in the house except for in here and within five feet of the front and back door. There's a patio off the family room. You can go as far as the overhang."

She tried to make herself feel better by thinking that at least an alarm sounding was better than him blowing off her hand, but she wasn't all that comforted. Tanner might be her only shot at staying alive, but she'd just exchanged one prison for another.

"My rules," he repeated.

"I got that."

She had a choice. She could accept them or she could be returned to Christopher. On second thought, not much of a choice at all.

For the first time since she'd been kidnapped, she had the overwhelming urge to cry. She wanted to slump down on the floor and sob until everything was better. Instead she sucked in a breath and forced herself to stay strong. Tanner was her only hope. She needed him on her side. He seemed to appreciate strength, so that's what she would show him.

"Anything else?" she asked, feeling her exhaustion down to her bones.

"No. Your room is down here."

He led her along another hallway before turning into a cheery bedroom. There was a full-size bed, a dresser with a television on it, two nightstands and a small desk. One door led into a closet, the other to a small bathroom, complete with a shower.

Madison had only been allowed to bathe every third

day while she'd been kidnapped. She longed for some serious water time. But first, sleep.

He glanced at his watch. "Why don't you rest for three or four hours. Then you can eat."

"Fine."

He walked to the door, then paused and turned back to her. "No phone, no contact with the outside world."

She wasn't even surprised. "So you could kill me and no one would ever know where I'd been or where to find the body."

His dark gaze settled on her face. "That's right."

"Good to know."

That bit of bravado took her last ounce of strength. When he left, she collapsed on the bed and let the tears flow. She wanted to scream that this wasn't fair—that she hadn't asked for any of it. But what was the point? She was here, stuck, afraid for her life. There was no going back. Just forward. She would get through this because the alternative was to get dead, and she refused to let Christopher win.

She rolled onto her back and stared at the ceiling. She'd been right when she'd said that no one would ever know where she'd been. She'd already been gone for twelve days and apparently no one had alerted the police. No doubt Christopher had come up with a story to cover her absence.

Her father had known the truth, of course, but he would have left all the details to his son-in-law. Even now, with her supposedly free but not there, Christopher would probably say she was resting. Recovering her strength—a euphemism for something she didn't want to think about.

Her father would believe him because Blaine liked his world simple. Nothing beyond his lab mattered.

She fingered the bracelet on her left wrist. Somehow it transmitted her position in the house. Maybe it did other things. Tanner was certainly thorough.

Who was this man who obviously didn't like her in the least and yet offered to help her? Why did he care if she lived or died?

Maybe he didn't, she thought, rolling onto her side and closing her eyes. Maybe she simply wasn't allowed to get dead on his watch. Unless he decided to kill her himself.

He was a professional, she reminded herself. If he did want to take her out, it would be quick. A small comfort, but in her current situation, nearly the only one she had.

And until that moment, if it ever came, Tanner would keep her safe. She believed that down to her bones. While she was under his protection, nothing bad could happen to her. For the first time in a long time, she felt safe. Funny how a man who obviously despised her without bothering to get to know her could give her such a feeling of comfort.

Chapter 4

Tanner double-checked that the alarm system was activated, then settled into his office to get some work done. Every half hour or so, he glanced at the display screen, but Madison didn't move.

Sleep would do her good, he thought. She'd been through hell. He had a feeling things would get worse before they got better, but they would deal with that when it happened. For now it was enough that she rested. Later they would talk and he would get more information on Hilliard.

Speaking of which… He returned his attention to the computer file he'd begun to build. Access to personal financial records could take a day or so. In the meantime, he filled in what he could about the man's past.

An hour later someone rang the bell. Tanner glanced

at the security-camera monitor and recognized the man standing on the front porch. Angel was right on time.

"What's the word?" he asked, after letting the other man into the house.

Angel, a tall, dark man with steely gray eyes and a scar that ran down his neck, shrugged. "Kelly's holding his own. He survived the surgery. Doc says that's good. Now we wait and see if he recovers. He lost a lot of blood."

"Brain damage?"

"They don't know yet."

"Odds?"

Angel shrugged again. "I didn't want to hear anything bad so I didn't ask."

Tanner wouldn't have, either. He took the wrapped package Angel offered, then asked, "You okay with the Calhoun job?"

"Sure thing. We've got three teams on the kid. Full-time. His crazy uncle isn't getting anywhere close." Angel's eyes brightened with interest. "If he does, I'll take him down."

Jefferson Alexander Calhoun III, was all of seven and an orphan. His parents had been killed in circumstances that could only be labeled suspicious, although the local police hadn't put together a case yet. The boy's maternal grandmother was concerned her youngest son had done it to make sure he inherited the bulk of the family fortune. She'd hired Tanner's company to protect the life of her only grandchild.

"If you have to take him out, make sure you're on the correct side of the law," Tanner reminded his right-hand man.

Angel smiled slowly. "I wouldn't do it any other way."

They discussed other jobs for a few more minutes, then Angel left. Tanner appreciated that the other man hadn't asked about Tanner's unexpected guest or the contents of the package. Tanner wasn't sure he could explain either. He was working based on very few facts but a strong feeling in his gut.

Hell of a way to do business, he thought as he dumped the package on a kitchen counter, then returned to his office to continue with his research.

Two hours later, he took a break to shower and change his clothes. When he walked back into the control room, he saw Madison was up and moving around. He detoured by the kitchen, grabbed the package and walked to her bedroom.

He found her standing on the desk chair, inspecting the moldings attached to the ceiling. She stood on tiptoe, her expression intense, her fingers probing every inch of the painted wood.

"It's not fancy, I'll admit," he said, "but I thought it looked decent enough. Are you disagreeing with me?"

Madison jumped when she heard his voice and turned on the chair. "What? You startled me."

He jerked his head toward the wall. "What's the problem?"

"I'm looking for the cameras," she said. "Is there anywhere in this room where I can go and not be watched?"

It took him a couple of seconds to make sense of her words. When he did, anger quickly followed.

"You think I'm spying on you?" he asked, annoyance tightening his voice.

She'd slept hard—her hair was mussed and there was a crease in her right cheek. She was wrinkled, in need of a shower and still pretty sleep deprived. But she stared back with a defiance that earned his grudging respect.

"What else should I think?" she asked, shaking her bracelet-clad wrist at him. "This place is more secure than my local bank vault. You've got a computer telling me where I can and can't go. Special screens on the windows so I can't escape. I'm your prisoner. Why wouldn't you spy on me?"

"Because I don't need to get my rocks off by watching you prance around in your underwear."

He dropped the package on the bed, crossed to the chair and grabbed her around the waist. Before she could react, he'd lowered her to the ground. He had a brief impression of heat and a too-thin body lacking curves before he released her and stepped away.

She glared at him. "I could have gotten down on my own."

"I'm sure you could have."

He took her hand in his and dragged her out of the room. She sputtered in protest but didn't pull away. As they approached the control room, he pulled a remote from his pocket and hit a button to deactivate the system. Then he brought her to the control panel, released her hand and pointed.

She rubbed her fingers and ignored the monitor. "Is there a reason you don't try asking me to go with you first? I assure you my intent is to cooperate. There's no need to be dragging and lifting all the time."

"Are you complaining about your treatment?"

"Yes."

"So noted."

Her gaze narrowed, and he could tell she wondered if the notation meant anything. He decided to keep her guessing about that, if nothing else.

"You're not looking," he said, still pointing to the monitor.

"At what?" She turned slowly and stared at the screen.

The picture showed a floor plan of the house, with all the rooms labeled. Exactly in the center of the room named Control Center stood a red dot.

"I'm the dot?" she asked.

"Walk around and find out."

She did as he suggested, moving to the window, then back toward the door. The dot on the screen moved with her.

Her attention shifted from the computer to him. "No pictures?" she asked.

"Not even a camera."

"I'm transmitting to that screen through the bracelet?"

He nodded.

"Oh." She glanced down at her wrist, then back at him. "It was a logical conclusion."

Her eyes were blue. He'd registered the fact before but hadn't paid any attention to them. Now he saw they were a deep, true color. She was pale—maybe from lack of sleep or food. Whatever the reason, her scar seemed more pronounced. Again he wondered why she hadn't gotten it fixed.

She had the kind of hair teenage boys daydreamed

about—straight, long and blond. Even with the scar she was beautiful. Not that he was interested.

"Logical," he agreed. "But I'm not the kind of guy who likes to watch."

Her delicate eyebrows rose. "I thought all men were into that."

He allowed himself a smile. "Maybe under different circumstances. Not like this."

"Good to know." She glanced around the room. "Do I get to find out what this equipment is for?"

"It's computers mostly. Some tracking equipment. I have a monitoring system for the house."

"No one gets in, no one gets out?"

"Not on my shift."

She walked to the window and looked out. He knew the view was little more than some lawn and a high fence topped with razor wire.

"Do you live here?" she asked, still looking out.

"No. I told you, it's a safe house."

"Who else do you bring here?"

"Sorry. That information is classified."

"Of course." She nodded. "But it does make me wonder. What exactly do you do with your life that you *own* a house like this?"

"I prepare in advance for whatever my clients might need."

She walked back toward him. "Who's your client now? Me? Christopher?"

"I'm winging it."

"You don't strike me as the kind of man who does that often."

He shrugged. "I try to be flexible."

Their eyes met. He read questions in hers. No fear, though, which he respected. She wasn't what he'd thought. Maybe not as useless as most women like her. She had backbone and more than a little—

He felt it then. Subtle at first, but growing. It filled the room, pressing in on him, stealing air, heating breath.

Awareness.

Of her. The scent of her skin, the way she moved. In the blink of an eye she went from someone he had to protect to a woman.

Dammit all to hell, he thought grimly. This was not allowed. He didn't get involved with clients. Not ever.

"I got you some clothes," he said and retraced his steps to the kitchen.

He heard her follow. When she'd cleared the control room, he hit the remote to reset the security system, then stopped by the package.

"One of my men came by with it," he told her.

She looked confused. "I don't understand."

"What's so complicated? I sent one of my guys to your place to get you some things."

"A man was in my condo?"

She sounded more surprised than outraged. Tanner pushed the package toward her.

"I doubt he spent a lot of time in your underwear drawer. You've been wearing what you have on for days. I thought you'd like something clean."

"I do. Thank you. I'm just not sure… How did he get in? What if Christopher is watching the building?"

"I'm guessing your ex had someone there. Don't worry. No one saw Angel."

"And how did he get in?"

Tanner shrugged. "He has his ways. Go on—" he pointed to her room "—take a shower, change your clothes. Then we'll eat. I have a lot of questions I need to ask you about your ex-husband."

"Sure. Okay." She picked up the package, then smiled. "Thanks."

With that, she walked down the hall. Tanner waited until she disappeared before heading into the control room. He watched the small red dot move on the screen. When it eased from the bedroom to the bathroom, he had to force himself to keep his attention on work and not on the thought of a naked woman stepping into the shower.

A three-hour nap and a shower had gone a long way to perking up Madison. The guy Tanner had sent to her house had brought back the basics—jeans, T-shirts, a couple of nightgowns and a few toiletries. She tried not to freak out at the thought of a strange man going through her underwear drawer and reminded herself that after all she'd been through, having a stranger grabbing bras and panties was the least of her problems.

After washing out the panties and bra she'd been wearing for the past ten days, she dried her hair. As she put away her blow-dryer, she realized she could smell something cooking. The delicious scent of tomato sauce and garlic had her mouth watering and her stomach growling. She felt like a cartoon animal floating along on the smell as she followed the scent down the hall and into the kitchen.

Tanner stood at the stove. He turned as she entered and smiled. She wasn't sure what shocked her more—that he was cooking or the smile itself. Both were unexpected, although the curve of his mouth made her uneasy in ways she couldn't define.

"Nothing fancy," he told her. "Spaghetti, meat sauce and a salad."

Her stomach growled again. She suddenly felt faint with hunger. "At this point I'd eat anything."

He jerked his head toward the table. "Then have a seat."

The round table had already been set with place mats, napkins and flatware. She settled in a chair just as he brought over a large bowl of pasta and another of salad.

"What do you want to drink?" he asked. "We have all the basics."

"Just water," she answered, as her stomach tightened in anticipation of food.

"Dig in," he told her.

She decided to take him at his word. She scooped up a large serving of the meat-covered pasta and dumped it on her plate. Salad could wait—right now she wanted something substantial.

The first bite was heavenly. The perfect blend of spices, the tender yet firm pasta. She couldn't chew fast enough.

Tanner returned with a bottle of water and set it next to her plate. She nodded her thanks but didn't stop eating. It was only after she'd finished the serving of pasta and reached for the salad that she glanced at him.

"Sorry to be such a pig."

"Don't sweat it." He took the seat opposite hers and served himself some pasta. "Why didn't you eat while you were kidnapped? Did you think a hunger strike would get their attention?"

She shrugged, choosing not to read any criticism into his words. "I never planned on avoiding food. For the first couple of days I was too scared to eat. Every time I tried, it wouldn't stay down. Eventually I was able to handle very small portions. A half a slice of toast in the morning. A cup of soup in the afternoon. Some people eat more when they're stressed—I eat less. Those people didn't believe me when I told them. They threatened to feed me themselves, using force, but it never came to that."

He studied her as she spoke. She would love to know what he was thinking, but then again, maybe not. Tanner had made it clear she wasn't his favorite person on the planet. Why hear more of the same?

They ate in silence. She had two servings of salad and three of pasta. When she'd finished, she leaned back in her chair and sighed.

"Better?" he asked.

She nodded. "Much. Thanks for cooking. You did a great job."

He smiled again. "Yeah, I can boil up pasta better than almost anyone."

The humor intrigued her. So far, her host had been all business. The smile softened his expression and added light to his eyes. It almost made him approachable. He was still dangerous, but it was nice to know there was a regular person under all that killer edge.

"I have some questions," he said. "I want to get as much information on your ex-husband as possible. The more you tell me, the more it will help with the investigation."

"Absolutely. I'll tell you everything."

The smile faded as if it had never existed and the warrior returned. He grabbed a notepad from the counter.

"Start at the beginning," he said. "Where did you and Hilliard meet?"

Chapter 5

"My father brought Christopher home for dinner one evening," Madison said. "They'd met at a conference. Christopher was very impressive. His parents had been killed while he was still in graduate school, but he'd managed to get his Ph.D. and run the family firm at the same time. My father admired his talent, his work ethic."

Tanner scribbled some notes. "What did you admire?"

"Excuse me?"

"You married the guy. You must have liked something you saw."

Right. Of course. Madison considered the question and wondered how to answer it. For her, those days were a lifetime ago. Maybe someone else's lifetime.

"I was a different person back then," she said slowly. Tension filled her body. Rather than sit and feel awkward, she stood and began to clear the table. "Different things impressed me. Christopher was smart and charming and sophisticated. He swept me off my feet. We were engaged two months after we met, and married three months after that. I didn't get to know the real man until sometime later."

"Who is the real man?"

Nothing in Tanner's voice gave away what he was thinking. Madison rinsed the dishes and loaded the dishwasher as she tried to form an answer.

How could she explain what was only a feeling?

"He has a dark side. He likes to gamble. He could drop a million dollars at a table and not even blink. He also has a temper. He can fly into a rage without warning." She was careful to speak without actually dwelling on the past. She didn't want to disappear into those memories.

"People tended to cross him only one time. He made sure they didn't do it twice," she said.

"Interesting, but not exactly the characteristics of someone willing to kidnap or kill."

She dried her hands on a towel and faced him. "You don't believe me?"

"I need more than this. Tell me about his company. You said he took it over when his parents died. How did they die?"

She rinsed the pasta pot, then put it on the top shelf of the dishwasher. "A car accident. They'd gone away skiing and they lost control of their car on an icy road."

"Was there any investigation into their deaths?"

"What? No. Why would there be?"

"If you think Hilliard is capable of having you kidnapped and killed, why not do away with his parents, too?"

"But he…" The thought stunned her. Was it possible? Could he have done that? "I don't know," she said honestly. "Maybe he could have."

"Tell me about your father's company."

She wiped off the counters, then returned to the table. "Adams Electronics makes tracking equipment for the military. As soon as someone creates a stealth technology, someone else tries to figure out a way to make it obsolete. My father's company has several contracts with the military. They bring him different foreign technologies and he finds a way around them."

"But the family fortune can't all come from military contracts."

"It doesn't. There are usually by-product discoveries, and that's where the real money comes from."

Tanner continued to write. His impersonal, professional manner made it easier for her to think about the past. It was more distant with him around, plus there was no way Christopher could find her here.

"You're the only child," he said, more a statement than a question.

"Yes. I'm sure my father wanted more children. Certainly a son to carry on in his footsteps. I was never very interested in the family business. I don't have the math gene."

"Not everyone does. Your mother?"

Madison leaned back in her chair and folded her arms over her chest. "She's, um, dead. It's been about ten years. She didn't have the math gene, either, although she could trace her lineage back to the Mayflower. Very east-coast old money, old family. My father was an upstart scientist who stole her away from her Ivy League fiancé."

"What does his family do?"

Madison frowned. "The old boyfriend?"

"Yeah."

"He's in construction. Skyscrapers and hotels."

"So there's nothing to connect him to this situation?"

"No."

"So what's Hilliard into that's so hot?" he asked.

"Some kind of innovative jamming technology. What I'm hearing is that it's the first jamming device that can't be defeated. So if someone were trying to track, say, your plane, and you were able to jam their radar signals, you could fly virtually invisible."

"Get a fighter jet right over D.C. and no one would know?"

"Exactly."

"Powerful."

"If it happens, it's going to be worth millions."

Tanner tapped the pen. "Maybe worth enough to kill for."

She didn't want to think about that.

"Is he smart enough to do it?" Tanner asked.

"I don't know. My father thinks so. He's been very excited about the project for over a year now." Blaine had always mentioned it when she'd first tried to talk about why she was leaving Christopher. As if her husband's brilliance was reason enough to stay.

"If Hilliard builds it, can your father figure out how to work around it?"

"He didn't seem very confident about the possibilities."

"Is he in on the deal with Hilliard?"

She knew what he meant. Were the two men working together to create more interest? Blaine Adams saying there was a technology he couldn't defeat was like Santa Claus announcing that he'd given up the toy business.

"I don't want to believe that about my father," she said quietly. "He's a good man. A little forgetful when it comes to interpersonal relationships, but not about his business. He has integrity."

"Which doesn't mean he can't be bought."

"Money isn't important to him."

Tanner wanted to believe her. She looked so damned earnest, sitting there all stiff and defiant. But he couldn't ignore a possibility just because it got her panties in a twist.

"If Hilliard has so much money, why doesn't he pay his bills?" he asked.

"I don't know. It's almost a point of honor with him. Like he's getting away with something. Most people aren't willing to take him on. They just grumble. There have been a couple of lawsuits, but they always get dropped."

She wasn't painting a picture of a very nice guy, Tanner thought. How had Hilliard swept her off her feet?

She leaned forward and rested her forearms on the table. "How is that man? The one who works for you and was injured."

Concern darkened her eyes and pulled at her mouth. Tanner didn't want to think about Kelly or the fact that the kid might not recover. He didn't want to have to make that phone call to his family or miss the kid himself.

"Holding his own. He survived the surgery."

"I'm sorry he was injured."

"You didn't shoot him."

"But it's still—"

He didn't want to talk about it so he said, "If your theory of Hilliard kidnapping you for the ransom money is right, then he's got to be pissed he missed out on his twenty million."

She perked up. "He didn't get the money?"

"I had it intercepted and returned directly to your father. Last I heard, it was already back in his account."

"I'm glad," she said fiercely.

"What would he need the money for?"

"Gambling debts."

"He's not in that deep."

"How do you know?" she asked.

"I checked."

"Then I don't know. Is he buying someone off for something? Maybe he stole the technology he's claiming as his own."

"Or buying it," Tanner said, focused more on the way Madison fingered the scar on her face. "How did that happen?"

She dropped her hand to her lap and stared at the table. "I don't remember. I know that sounds strange, but it's true. I can't figure out if I hit my head or if I've just blocked out the memory. I was fighting with Christopher. This was before I left him. He'd been badgering me about my work and wanting me to quit."

Tanner stared at her. "You have a job?"

"Yes. I don't get paid—I'm a volunteer—but I'm expected to show up every day to get things done." She raised her gaze to his. "I'm not completely useless."

The jury was still out on that one, he thought. "Let me guess. No wife of his should hold a job."

"Exactly. He and my father ganged up on me. They said I should stay home and focus on being a good wife. That I wasn't…strong enough to do both."

Strong enough? He might not be a Madison Hilliard fan, but he was more than convinced of her determination and will.

"My father left," she continued. "Christopher kept yelling at me. I know he slapped me, but then it all gets blurry."

"Is that the first time he hit you?" Tanner asked, knowing the information was significant. When men beat their wives, the situation often escalated into murder.

"Yes."

He waited, staring her down.

"It was the first time," she told him. "And one of the reasons I left."

"Fair enough. So did you fall when he hit you?"

"No. I just stood there and stared at him. He was yelling. I'm not sure he knew what he'd done."

"He knew." Men always knew when they hit a woman.

"Okay. The next thing I remember is kneeling on the ground. I'd somehow gone through the glass door. I was bleeding." She touched her cheek again. "I honestly can't tell you if he pushed me or if I tripped or what."

Tanner would put money on the bastard pushing her

or throwing her. He wasn't surprised Madison had blocked the memory. No one would want to find out that her husband was a monster.

"He stood over me, still yelling, but he seemed happy, too. He said I would be as ugly as the children I tried to help. That I'd earned that. Then he was gone. I drove myself to the emergency room. The doctor there stitched me up and sent me home. When I got back, Christopher was gone. I remember feeling grateful. I spoke to an attorney the next day to find out what divorcing him would involve. It took me a couple of months to get the courage to leave, but I did it."

Tanner looked at his notes because staring at Madison had become too much of an invasion of her privacy.

"What kind of children do you work with?" he asked.

"Poor children with facial deformities. The charity I'm involved with arranges for them and their parents to be flown here for reconstructive surgeries. We pay for everything, even the follow-up care they need back home." She smiled. "The kids are so amazing. I guess they're all tough because they've had to endure so much growing up. It's great when we can help a baby or a toddler, but the older kids will break your heart."

Her face changed as she spoke. Her expression softened and her eyes filled with wonder.

"My job is to coordinate the travel plans to and from their homes and to make sure all the medical services are lined up. While the family is here, I'm their point of contact."

Is that why she kept the scar? So the kids could see she was one of them?

As soon as the thought registered, he pushed it away. No one was that altruistic—certainly not as beautiful a woman as Madison.

"We try to make their trip as much of an adventure as possible," Madison continued. "If we can fit it in, we like to take them to Disneyland and on a studio tour. I make sure the moms get a spa day." She smiled. "You can't know what a difference it makes to be normal. To not be laughed or pointed at or run from."

She was a believer. He heard it in her voice. She actually gave a damn about those kids.

"How did you get involved?" he asked.

"It was just a quirk of fate," she told him. "I was at a low point in my life. Oh, yeah, the rich girl was depressed because she wasn't happy. How sad." She shook her head. "I was an idiot. I was also walking to try to clear my head. I came upon a woman and her daughter on a bus bench. They were both crying. Normally I would never have gotten involved, but there was something about them. Something I couldn't ignore. So I went over and asked if I could help."

She sipped from her bottle of water. "It turns out the woman and her daughter were from Oregon. Lacey— that was the little girl—had a cleft palate. They'd come down for the surgery, taking the bus, but when they got here, no one knew anything about an operation. I don't know if their application got lost or what. They didn't have any money or anywhere to stay. They were given a voucher for a night at a hotel and a return ticket, but that wasn't what they'd come for."

She put down the bottle. "I took them to the hotel and

then went to the charity. It took a couple of days, but in the end, Lacey got her surgery and I found my calling."

He could feel her enthusiasm and energy. She kept surprising him. "You like what you do," he said.

"No. I love it. It's my reason for living. After I left Christopher, I threw myself into my work." She glanced at him. "I've been out of touch for nearly two weeks."

"You're not going into your office."

"I know. I can't risk that, but I thought maybe I could use a computer and do some work on the Internet. If I could just have access to my e-mail..."

"No."

"What would it hurt?"

"My game," he reminded her. "My rules."

"Well, your rules suck. I'm not asking to buy shoes at the Nordstrom's Web site. I want to be in touch with my kids."

"No."

She slammed both hands on the table and glared at him. "You're being stubborn and there's no reason to be. This is important. This matters. You have no idea what it's like to grow up different and ugly and deformed."

"You don't know anything about me," he said.

She laughed then. A bright, clear sound that hit him in the gut like a sucker punch. "Oh, please, Tanner. Look in the mirror. You're good-looking and powerful. You probably always have been." Her humor faded. "These kids aren't. They're misfits who are laughed at on a daily basis. They need me and I'm going to be there for them. If my being out of touch means even one child doesn't get his or her surgery, then none of this is worth it."

"A pretty speech," he said, doing his best not to buy into her passion.

"I mean every word of it."

"Are you willing to risk your life for it?"

"Yes," she said without hesitation. "I'll do whatever you say. You can monitor my e-mail. You can even stand over me while I type. I don't care. But I need to have access to my mail and my files at work."

Suddenly uncomfortable, he stood and picked up his notes. "I'll think about it," he told her. "No promises."

Chapter 6

Madison slept through the night. It was the first time in nearly two weeks, and she felt like a new person when she woke up in the morning. After another long shower, luxuriating in the unlimited hot water and her access to shampoo and privacy, she dressed and went in search of coffee.

Not surprisingly, Tanner was already up. She passed him in the control room on her way to the kitchen.

He sat in front of the computer, typing something. The long-sleeved dark shirt of the previous day had been replaced with a black T-shirt. Impressive muscles stretched out the cotton.

If he was so busy being commando-guy and saving the world, when did he find the time to work out? Because he had to—no guy was so physically perfect without a little effort.

"Morning," he said when she paused a few feet from the doorway. "You're up early."

She glanced at the clock on the wall. It was a little after seven. "I guess I'm anxious to start my day." Not that she had all that much planned to occupy her time. Now if she had her computer…

But that was a conversation to have after coffee, she thought as she smiled politely and continued to the kitchen, where a pot stood at the ready.

After pouring a cup, she settled on one of the kitchen chairs and glanced through the newspaper Tanner had left. But she couldn't seem to make sense of the words—probably because she felt too unsettled.

It was the circumstances, she told herself. Stress. She'd been through a lot in the past couple of weeks and now she was living with a man she didn't know, in a place no one else knew about. While she didn't think Tanner would kill her and hide the body, she wasn't used to being so in the dark about her future.

Then there was the man himself. She could rarely figure out what he was thinking. He seemed to despise her only a little less than he had before. She wondered if she was crazy to trust him, then winced at her word choice.

No, she told herself. Not crazy. Under the circumstances, trusting Tanner only made sense.

She was still working on convincing herself when he walked into the kitchen to pour himself more coffee. She watched his easy movements, the bunch and release of muscles. In another world, at another time, she would have found him attractive and intriguing. Now he was just a mystery.

"Why are you doing this?" she asked.

He glanced from her to the pot he held. "I like coffee."

She held in a smile. "No, why are you helping me?"

"I was hired to rescue you, not turn you over to a potential killer. Until I know it's safe to let you go, I'll keep you here."

Pretty much what she'd figured. "A man of honor?" she asked.

"That's pushing it."

"But you're doing the right thing."

He raised his eyebrows. "That has yet to be determined."

"So you think I could still be lying."

"About some things. You were right about Hilliard not paying his bills. He has a long trail of angry creditors. A few of them have pursued legal action."

"I told you that," she reminded him. "The lawsuits were dismissed."

"Not all of them, and not necessarily for legal reasons."

She didn't like the sound of that. "Meaning?"

"Sometimes the person pursuing the suit disappeared."

Her chest tightened and she tasted fear. "He doesn't like people who get in his way," she said, hating to have that confirmed.

"Apparently not."

"I know he's a threat to me. What about my father?" she asked.

"Hilliard needs him."

"For now."

Tanner shrugged.

"Can you protect him?" she asked. "Would you let

me hire you to do that? If you could get a couple of guys into the company, just to hang around him…"

"I'll check into it."

"I can pay you."

He sipped his coffee. "I'm not questioning that."

Some of her tension eased. If Tanner would look after her father, she wouldn't have to worry about him. Sure, Christopher needed Blaine in the short term, but for how long? And then what?

"I hate this," she said. "I hate that he's in my life. Just thinking about him makes my skin crawl."

"For what it's worth, he didn't go to the police about me keeping you here," Tanner said. "He also hasn't tried to get in touch with me."

She let the news sink in. "If my ex-husband didn't go to the authorities about you holding on to me, that has to mean something."

"It's helping your case," he admitted.

"You're a very stubborn man."

"I'm careful."

If he kept her alive, she wasn't going to complain about his need to be cautious.

"I'm going to go crazy here with nothing to do," she said. "I think we should argue about my computer again."

He surprised her by smiling. "You willing to take me on?"

She swallowed more coffee before offering a brazen, "Absolutely."

"What if you piss me off so much that I won't help you?"

She dismissed the suggestion with a shrug. "You

kept me here and safe, even though you don't like me. I doubt annoying you about my computer is going to make a difference. You don't operate that way."

"How do I operate?"

"I'm not completely sure, but I know you're not slimy."

He studied her for several minutes before speaking. "I reserve the right to review your e-mail. I'll also download your hard disk and look it over."

Relief swept through her. "Read it all twice, I don't care. I just want to get back to work. I have a laptop at home."

"I figured. I'll have one of my men stop by and pick it up. If you want anything else from the condo, write it down."

Madison held in a whoop of delight. When Tanner walked out of the kitchen, she found a pen and paper, then wrote out a quick list. She headed for the control room and hovered outside.

"Here it is," she said, holding it out for him.

Tanner put his computer to sleep, grabbed the keys and stepped into the hallway. He took the paper and read it over, then nodded.

"I'll be back in a couple of hours."

He was leaving? She didn't know if that was good or bad. "Okay."

"Don't try to run away. Don't try to go outside or into the control room. If you do, the alarm will be set off and I'll be paged. You're not going to get out of here without me, and if you try, all bets are off. Do I make myself clear?"

As she had no intention of leaving, it was easy to agree. Five minutes later, he was gone and she was alone.

When she heard the garage door automatically close, she walked directly to the phone and picked it up. Instead of a dial tone, she heard a computerized voice asking for her access code.

"Why am I not surprised," Madison murmured as she made her way into the family room and picked up the remote for the television. She was well and truly Tanner's prisoner. It seemed like a good time to check out daytime TV.

Tanner typed computer keys while Madison hovered impatiently in the hallway. He couldn't see her directly, but he caught most of her movements out of the corner of his eye.

"You're bugging me," he told her, not looking up from his work.

"Could you be slower?" she asked with obvious impatience. "How long does it take to copy a stupid disk drive?"

"It takes longer when you're distracting me."

She pressed her lips together but continued her fidgety, shuffling almost dance.

"I'll have Internet access, right?" she asked. "You said I would."

"Yes. High-speed and everything. Your e-mail will be monitored."

"Whatever," she told him. "It's just work stuff. You're not going to find me having cybersex with anyone."

"Good to know. I was more concerned about you telling a friend you're in hiding. You'll have to tell them you're recovering from the flu at a friend's house. Or staying out of town."

"Oh. Right." She actually stood still for a full five seconds. "You don't want our position compromised."

He looked up and glared at her. "This isn't a war movie."

She gave him a cheeky grin. "Maybe not, but we do have a position to compromise. Don't worry, Captain. I'll take the secret information to my death."

"How much coffee have you had?"

"Way too much. I was bored. I did lousy on all the game shows I watched while you were gone, but I got some great ideas for a faux finish for the kitchen walls on a decorating show. Want to hear?"

"No."

He stood and carried her laptop to her. She grabbed it and clutched it to her chest.

"Thank you, thank you, thank you," she said happily. "I promise to be a good little computer user." Her humor faded a little. "Christopher won't be able to trace me back here, will he? He's kind of a computer geek. It's a hobby with him."

"You're untraceable. Even if he figures out a way to know when you're online, any trace will turn up false addresses. As far as he and the rest of the world are concerned, this place doesn't exist."

"Good to know. Seriously, thanks for this. I'm back in business."

She twirled in the hallway, then hurried to her room. Tanner watched her go. Her long hair fluttered out behind her and her snug jeans outlined the faint curve of her hips.

She needed a good twenty pounds packed on her before she could escape being called bony, but she had some potential. Not that he would do anything about it. Number one, she wasn't his type. Number two, while she was his responsibility, he wouldn't try anything. Number three, he doubted she was interested in what he had in mind.

Just as well, he told himself. Women like her made things complicated. He would bet a lot of money that Madison had never had sex just for the sake of it. That to her the act was as emotional and spiritual as physical. The thought of which made him tired.

He returned to the control room and sat in front of his computer. While he would rather be beaten than admit it, he was starting to like her. She was nothing he'd imagined and nothing like other rich women he'd met. She seemed to have values and a sense of someone other than herself.

Which could all be an act, he reminded himself as he began to type. Although he would know soon enough. A quick trip through her computer would tell him if her work was as important to her as she claimed.

Stanislav was not a big man. Barely five foot eight with a thin build, he looked like the guy you pushed around on the beach. Christopher knew better. He'd seen the Russian cut off a man's hand, fingers first, then the thumb, then finally slicing the rest off at the wrist. That man had stolen less than a hundred dollars from one of Stanislav's gambling clubs.

Now, as Stanislav walked around his office, picking

up pieces of art, admiring pictures, Christopher felt sweat trickle down his back. He kept his attention on the smaller Russian man when he really wanted to stare at Stanislav's very large, very stoic associates.

"Very nice," Stanislav said with only the slightest of accents. "I like your office. You find it very creative, yes?"

"Uh, yeah. Sure. It's great. But this is mostly for guests. I do the real work down in the lab."

Stanislav turned to look at him. The Russian's pale blue eyes seemed to be made of ice. "By 'real work' you mean taking what I give you, taking our technology and pretending to make it your own."

Christopher swallowed, not sure what to say. "I, uh…"

Stanislav waved him to silence.

"You Americans," he began as he walked to the floor-to-ceiling window and stared out at the view of Brentwood. "You think you are so superior. That we are a backward country with no creativity. No spark. Yet who do you come to for your technology? Where do you try to buy the next big thing?" He turned and glared at Christopher. "Russia. *Our* scientists created the jamming device you want so badly. In their small back rooms and underground laboratories. We designed it, tested it and would have brought it to market." He drew his eyebrows together. "Or maybe we would have used it on you. We could have flown here on radar-invisible planes and crushed you while you slept."

"You sure could have," Christopher said, doing his best to keep his voice from shaking.

Stanislav moved close. "But we did not," he said from only a foot away. His pale gaze locked on Christopher's face. "We became what we are today—a broken country going nowhere. For some, this is better. Better for me. In the new order I am a rich, powerful man. But not better for Russia. Still, what is done is done."

Christopher nodded as fear swelled inside of him.

"I came to you because of your reputation," Stanislav said, his voice low. "Because of who you were and the business I thought we could do together. I trusted you."

"I appreciate that," Christopher said quickly. "I want to do what I can to keep that trust."

"Then where is the goddamn money?" Stanislav asked in a roar.

Christopher flinched and stepped back. Instantly two of the three associates were at his side, holding him in place. He felt their strong fingers digging into his arms and knew he was well and truly trapped.

"You think I don't know what this technology is worth?" Stanislav asked, his temper back under control. "When your company finishes producing the first prototype, you will be able to jam any radar system in the world. This is power. This is the future. Your company will make billions the first year."

The Russian's pale eyes narrowed. "And yet, on the verge of that, you try to trick me."

Oh, God. No! Fear turned to panic. "Not that," Christopher said, picturing that other man and his hand. The blood and the screams as each finger was slowly cut off.

"I'm not trying to trick you," he said earnestly. "I would never do that. Never. I swear. I'll get the money. I had a plan. A good plan. But somebody got in my way."

Stanislav stared at him. "What was your plan?"

Christopher hesitated, not sure how the other man would react to the truth. The hands holding him tightened.

"I kidnapped my ex-wife and convinced her father to cough up fifteen million in ransom." There was no point in mentioning the five million he owed in gambling money.

The Russian's expression didn't change. Christopher braced himself for the worst when the other man began to laugh. The associates let him go. The relief was so strong, it made his legs tremble. He forced himself to stay upright.

Stanislav slapped Christopher on the back. "Your own wife? Good for you. You could almost be Russian. So what went wrong?"

"The guy I hired turned out to be too good. His men intercepted the ransom money before I could collect it."

The humor faded as if it had never been. "For so intelligent a man, you make many mistakes," Stanislav said. "I don't like that."

"I know. I'm sorry." If he got his hands on Tanner, he would kill him, Christopher vowed.

Stanislav glanced at his men, then back at Christopher. "One week, my friend. Only because we have come so far and it would take time to find another buyer. But be warned. No more excuses. If you do not have the money in a week, I will kill you. But first I will make you wish you were dead."

Christopher believed him.

"I'll have it," he said.

Stanislav shrugged, as if to say it hardly mattered, then he walked out and his associates followed.

Christopher sank down into the chair in front of his desk and tried to catch his breath. One week. What could he do in a week?

Robbing a bank came to mind, and if he thought he could pull it off and get enough money, he would have started planning. But the outcome was too questionable. Better to go for the sure thing. Which meant Blaine Adams.

They'd been talking about merging the companies. Obviously it was time to resurrect those discussions and then leak word to the press. That would be enough to push up stock prices. With the shares Christopher already owned of both companies and the options he had on his own, he might come close to his fifteen million.

If he'd gotten his hands on the ransom, none of this would be a problem. Somehow, some way he would make Tanner Keane pay for that. And for keeping Madison. If the bitch was here, he could force her to sign over her shares to him. That had to be at least ten million.

But she wasn't here. She'd managed to convince Keane that she was the innocent in all this. That he, Christopher, couldn't be trusted. He needed her.

But how to convince her it was safe to come home? And if he couldn't do that, how could he lure her out of hiding? There had to be a way.

Chapter 7

Tanner scanned the files in Madison's computer. The work was fairly easy. She didn't keep any financial records on the machine or use it for more than correspondence, setting up schedules, her appointment calendar and e-mail.

He found that she'd told the truth about her work. She really did help kids with facial deformities. In her document files there were folders for each child she'd dealt with. The older files contained everything from copies of applications to travel arrangements and letters, including e-mails sent back and forth. There were also medical notes, follow-up reports and her own personal log of the child's time in Los Angeles.

He clicked on a file at random and scrolled through various documents. He stopped on an e-mail titled Big Fat Kissy Thank You.

Dear Madison—You have been more wonderful than I can ever say. I mean, the dress was so huge of you, but then to have Miss Cissy come and do my hair and everything. Wow! Mom says she's getting the pictures developed this weekend and we'll send you some.

I can't believe I finally got to go to my first ever dance. Brice was really cool and he brought me a corsage and it was so romantic. He even kissed me good-night.

Before, when I met you, I never thought a boy could ever like me. I was too ugly. But you said my life would change. You said I would be beautiful and you were right.

I love you so much and I don't know how to say thank you for what you've done. You're the best. I hope you have lots of kids of your own so you can love them just as much as you love me.

Your friend, Kristen.

Tanner stared at the screen for several seconds before closing the file. There was a response from Madison, but he didn't read it—he didn't need to. From what he'd seen so far, she was the genuine article. Someone who cared.

How was that possible? How could someone like her—rich, privileged, spoiled—ever look past her own small life into someone else's? She'd told him the story of seeing the woman and her child crying on a bus bench, but so what? How many other people had simply hurried by?

He turned in his chair to stare at the security screen. The dot that represented Madison sat motionless in the center of her room. No doubt she'd already logged on to the Internet to collect her e-mail.

In the past thirty-six hours, he'd pushed her, bullied her and threatened her. She'd taken it all and had come back for more. He'd yet to catch her in a lie. Maybe, just maybe, she was exactly who and what she said.

He wouldn't have thought it was possible. Beauty, brains and integrity?

His computer beeped. He glanced at the screen and saw a flag for outgoing mail. He'd already warned Madison that he would be monitoring her e-mail and he'd meant it. Now he clicked on the icon, then opened the file and scanned the letter she'd sent to her boss at the charity.

The text was innocuous. Madison claimed an ongoing family emergency kept her from her work, although she would be in touch via e-mail. She attached several open case files, asking for updates and offering to help in any way she could from home.

He read the e-mail twice before sending it on. There was a second letter to her assistant, asking for information on a burned toddler who had been brought out here for surgery.

Tanner sent that one on, as well, then continued his check of Madison's hard drive. At this point, he didn't expect to find anything, but he believed in being thorough.

* * *

Madison felt her spirits rise with each keystroke. After nearly two weeks of being out of touch, she felt great to finally connect with her kids and her staff.

She sat propped up on the bed as she dashed off a couple of e-mails explaining that she would continue to be away from the office for a while. One of the pluses of not being a paid employee was that her boss couldn't actually complain if she, Madison, had to be gone. Madison figured it was better to keep the story vague than to explain she'd been kidnapped.

Next she went through her in-box and sorted through the letters from children. She liked to stay in touch with her clients, hear about their lives and the positive changes brought on by reconstructive surgery.

There was an e-mail from Thomas, a little boy scarred by a gunshot. He told her all about his visit to his grandmother's house and how he played with the other kids in the neighborhood and that none of them made fun of him.

Madison touched the screen of her laptop and wished she could hold the precious child in her arms. If she ever got tired or frustrated or unhappy with her life, she only had to read these letters to have her world put back in perspective. If she—

Tanner walked into her bedroom. She glanced at him and was surprised when her heart gave a little flip of happiness.

Wait a minute. What was up with that? She couldn't possibly be attracted to Tanner. Sure, he was tall, dark and dangerous, which made him the female version of catnip, but so what? He despised her and she only wanted him around to keep her alive. They weren't about to get involved.

Before she could figure out what was going on, he stalked to the bed and threw several pieces of paper at her. She grabbed one and stared at it.

"What?" she asked.

"Explain these. You'd better talk fast because I'm about ready to take you back to your ex."

The threat chased away any lingering warm fuzzies. She grabbed the pages and tried to read them. Fear made it hard to concentrate, and she had to study each word until it made sense. When that happened, she knew she'd stepped into an alternate universe.

The e-mails were from her to Christopher, begging him to take her back. She pleaded, she bargained, she offered sexual favors that made her blush. When she'd finished the first one, she knew she didn't want to read any more, nor did she know what to say.

She could feel Tanner's fury filling the room. Whatever credibility she'd built up with him had just expired.

"I didn't write these," she told him, frantic with worry but without any idea as to how to convince him.

"They're on your computer."

"I figured that, but I didn't write them." She stared at the typewritten pages and wished they'd been written by hand. At least then she could demand handwriting analysis to prove her point. "I swear, it wasn't me."

"Then who?" he asked, obviously not interested in believing her. "Oh, wait. Let me guess. Your ex-husband broke into your condo, typed these on your computer and left them for me to find."

"Maybe." Although she knew it sounded improbable, it had to be true. Panic swelled inside of her. "Tanner, I didn't do this. I don't want anything to do with the man."

"Right." He turned to leave.

Madison knew he was her only hope. Without Tanner on her side, she was as good as dead. Maybe not right away, but as soon as Christopher didn't need her anymore.

She pushed aside her computer and scrambled to her feet to chase after him. She grabbed his arm before he could step into the hallway.

He glared down at her. "I told you not to take me for a fool. That I wasn't interested in any sick games you and your ex might want to play."

"I know. I'm not playing. I'm not doing anything. I'm the innocent bystander in all this."

His dark eyes were unreadable, but she felt his anger. Helplessness made her stomach tighten.

"I'll do anything," she said frantically. "Tell me how to prove my innocence. I'll sign anything. I'll—" a lightbulb went on "—I'll take a lie-detector test."

His gaze narrowed slightly. "They're not dependable."

"They have to be worth something."

"I prefer drugs."

She didn't know exactly what that meant. "Truth serum?"

"Something like that. Still interested in me finding out the truth?" Contempt filled his voice.

She dropped her hand to her side and swallowed. While the idea of being drugged so Tanner could probe her brain didn't make her want to do the happy dance, it beat the alternative of being returned to Christopher.

"All right," she said slowly. "You can drug me."

A muscle in his jaw tightened. "You won't have any control," he told her. "You won't be able to keep the truth from me. It's not a pleasant experience."

He sure wasn't going out of his way to make it any better, she thought grimly. "I doubt it is, but I can't think of another way to convince you I'm not lying. Can you?"

He shrugged as if he didn't care. Most likely, he didn't. As far as he was concerned, she'd tricked him. Tanner wasn't the sort of man to forgive that.

"So how does this happen?"

"I give you an injection, we wait twenty minutes, then we talk."

"All right. I have to shut down my computer."

"Come to the control room when you're done. You'll also want to go to the bathroom first."

Because why? But she didn't ask because she didn't want to know.

Tanner turned off the security system in the control room so Madison could enter without setting off the alarm. He crossed to the cabinet on the far wall and opened the metal door. In addition to office supplies, extra ammunition and communications equipment, the space also held a first-aid kit and several different drugs, including sedatives and chemicals known to make people willing to talk.

Tanner studied the options before picking up one small vial and tapping it. The powerful drug not only induced the patient to tell the truth, it erased the memory of the interrogation. For his purposes, even a very small dose had the side benefit of making the recipient feel woozy and spaced-out.

He set down the vial and stared out the window. He'd been furious when he'd found the letters. After finally deciding he could trust Madison, he'd had proof that she was jerking his chain. He'd been determined to get rid of her within the hour.

But her shock had been genuine and her willingness to do anything to prove that she hadn't written the letters made him willing to give her another chance.

What concerned him much more than her lying or not lying was that he gave a damn. His reaction to finding the letters had been personal. He'd felt as if she'd betrayed *him* and he didn't like that. Why should he care? She was a job, nothing more. Maybe she wasn't the useless, rich drama queen he'd first imagined, but she wasn't anyone he could like or respect.

Or was she? Was there any other explanation for his reluctance to drug her? It wasn't that he didn't want to hear the truth, it was that he didn't want her to feel sick and out of control. He cared about her reaction.

"You're losing it," he muttered to himself.

A flicker of movement on one of the monitors caught his attention. He saw Angel walking up to the front of the house. There was something about the grim expression on the other man's face that warned him the news wasn't good.

Tanner pulled open the door before Angel could knock.

"It's Kelly," Angel said flatly. "He died about an hour ago. Complications from the surgery. He never surfaced after the operation. I know you're busy here, so I've already talked to his family. Shari, his fiancée, was with him at the end, as was his mom."

Tanner felt the sharp pain lance through his gut. "He was a kid."

"Yeah. And a good soldier. We were lucky to have known him."

Tanner shook his head. "You tell the other men?"

"Not yet. I will. I wanted to let you know first."

"Okay. Thanks."

Angel nodded, then turned to leave. Tanner closed the door.

He'd known Kelly for over six years. The kid had come to him when he was barely twenty. He'd wanted a job because he thought the dangerous work was glamorous. Tanner had sent him away to grow up and get some seasoning. And to find out if Kelly was serious.

The kid was. Three years later, he'd returned after serving a tour in the Army. He'd seen action in Iraq and had left with a couple medals. Tanner had been impressed enough to offer him a temporary assignment. Kelly had proved himself and had joined the team.

Now he was dead—a kid cut down before he really had a chance to live—and all because something went wrong on what should have been a textbook operation.

"I'm ready," Madison said.

He hadn't heard her walk down the hall. Now he stared at her, at her elegant and expensive clothes, at her perfectly colored hair, and knew she was to blame. Rage filled him.

"He's dead," he said. "Kelly O'Neil. Irish. His family came over here nearly a hundred years ago. He has two sisters, a mother and a fiancée. He just got engaged. Shari, his fiancée, was with him when he died. There are death benefits, a life insurance policy. Not a whole hell of a lot of comfort to a family who just lost a twenty-six-year-old kid. He'll never get married, never have children, never grow old. And for what?"

Madison paled. "It's my fault."

"I couldn't agree more."

She started to speak, then turned and ran.

Chapter 8

Madison leaned against the tub and tried to catch her breath. Her stomach still rebelled, but she thought she was done vomiting. A shudder shot through her, making her curl into a ball. Every part of her ached—her heart most of all.

A man was dead because of her. She'd never thought she would ever have to think that, had never wanted to. The horror filled her until it was impossible to have any other thought. She tried to tell herself that it had been Christopher and his men, not her, but she had been the reason Kelly had been at that house in the first place.

She didn't know what to do, what to think. How could she atone for this? There were no words, no actions. A family had been destroyed forever because of her.

She pushed herself up so she could sit on the edge of

the tub. After covering her face with her hands, she waited for the tears, but there weren't any. It was as if her body felt completely numb, yet filled with too much pain to contain.

Slowly, awkwardly, she stood, then stumbled to the sink. After washing her face, she reached for the toothbrush and used it. It was only when she grabbed the hand towel that she saw Tanner reflected in the mirror. He stood just outside the bathroom. Waiting.

"Ready?" he asked calmly.

"What?"

"Are you ready to start the interrogation?"

She wasn't sure what frightened her more—the word *interrogation* or the coldness she saw in his eyes.

"I'm not going through with that now," she told him.

"You've already agreed. Backing out isn't an option."

Before she could protest, he grabbed her arm and pulled her out of the bedroom. She was too stunned to fight him, or maybe deep down she thought she deserved whatever he wanted to do. Maybe if she went along with it, she would be able to breathe again and not feel so horrible about what had happened to Kelly.

He led her to the control room. She crossed the threshold, then balked when she saw the table beside the chair and the vials and needles on the table.

"No!" She tried to twist free.

Tanner only tightened his grip on her. His fingers dug into her skin and made her wince. He guided her to the chair, then released her so suddenly that she stumbled into the seat. Seconds later her forearm was strapped to the arm of the chair.

This wasn't happening, she told herself. He couldn't be doing this.

"I trusted you," she told him.

His dark eyes didn't even flicker in response. "Big mistake." He picked up a vial and a needle.

Her heart pounded in her chest. She tried to pull free of the chair but couldn't. Somehow this had become about more than the letters. They were involved in a battle of wills and she knew she couldn't let him win.

Unfortunately she didn't seem to have any choice.

He dabbed her arm with a cotton ball soaked in rubbing alcohol. She inhaled the sharp scent and gave a strangled laugh.

"Oh, right. You're going to pump me full of chemicals that will screw with my mind, but God forbid I should get an infection."

The needle pierced her skin. She felt the momentary prick of pain, then nothing. No heat, no burning. Nothing.

"How long?" she asked.

"About twenty minutes."

Too much time to sit there wondering what it was going to feel like, she thought.

Tanner stepped back. She stared at the clock and started counting the seconds.

At first she didn't notice any change. Then gradually her body began to relax. She had the sense of getting lighter and lighter until she felt as if she could float away. In a way it was like being drunk, but with more intensity. Her body wasn't part of her anymore. He released her arm, but she couldn't move it.

Then he was there, in her face. He'd pulled up a chair so he was right in front of her.

Angry, she thought hazily. He was so very angry with her.

Tanner waited until Madison's eyes had fully dilated before beginning the questioning.

"Tell me your full name," he said.

"Madison Taylor Adams Hilliard. Taylor for my mother." She shook her head a little. "What was he thinking? He had to have known."

"What was who thinking?"

"My father. By the time I was born, he had to have known." She reached her fingers toward him but couldn't move her arm. "You're furious. I can see it shimmering around you. All sharp angles and knives. I'm sorry." Her voice dropped to a whisper. "I'm so sorry."

Tanner swore under his breath and looked at the needle on the table. He'd given her more than he'd planned. Or maybe not. Maybe after hearing about Kelly's death he'd wanted to put her at risk. And so he had. With her slight build, she wouldn't have much body mass to absorb the chemicals. She would get the full impact right away.

"Tell me about Christopher," he said, making his voice gentle. "You met at a party."

She swayed in her seat. "My father brought him. He was nice. Funny. He complimented me on the caterers. Most people compliment the hostess on the meal, but I never cooked. I liked that he got the irony of it all. He took time with me. He made me feel…strong."

An odd trait to cause someone to get married, he thought.

"Was he ever angry? Did he have a temper?"

She flinched. "Yes. Not at first. Not until after we were married. He didn't like how I spoke to the bartender on our honeymoon. He thought I was being too friendly. It wasn't about sex—she was a woman. But he didn't want me fraternizing with the staff. He said it didn't look right."

"What happened?"

"He yelled." Her blue eyes darkened with pain. "He didn't hit me. In a way, that was worse. He told me I was useless. That I couldn't do anything right. He told me he was sorry he'd married me, but he would stick it out because it was the right thing to do. I didn't feel strong anymore."

Tanner felt his anger begin to fade. "Did you love him?"

"No," she whispered, as if afraid Christopher would hear her and punish her. "At first I thought I did, but not for long. He frightened me. I tried not to let him know, but I think he guessed. Then I decided to ignore him and live my own life."

"When you got involved with the children?"

A smile pulled at the corner of her mouth. "Yes. With them."

"Are you glad you're divorced?"

Her expression turned fierce. "Yes. I'm sorry I ever married him. I'm sorry I bought into his lies. I don't even hate him. Hate would mean energy and caring, and I refuse to waste either on him. I simply want him out of my life."

"Did you ever write Christopher letters begging him to take you back?"

"No."

She spoke without hesitation, but he already knew the truth. Maybe he always had. His reaction to those letters had been visceral—as if someone he cared about had betrayed him. The unexpected emotion had caused him to react. Not exactly a moment to be proud of.

"I'm sorry," he said.

She sighed. "Don't be. You saved me. He's going to kill me, you know. Unless we can stop him. I think it's been his plan for a long time. He never forgave me for that family."

"What family?"

"The one I brought home." She shook her head and smiled. "Middlewood. I remember thinking it sounded so British, but they were from Mississippi. Cajun, mostly, but someone somewhere had picked up the last name. Little Jenny had been born with several bones missing in her face. I arranged the surgery, the transportation, all of it. But then there was a problem with the hotel and it was a holiday weekend and they had nowhere to go."

"What did you do?" he asked.

"Took them home with me. Christopher was *not* happy. He flew into a rage and screamed so long and so hard, I packed everyone up and drove east until I finally found us a hotel room in San Bernardino. I thought he was going to kill one of us."

She stared at him. "I knew then it was over. That the marriage was dead and if I didn't leave, I would be dead, too. Back then I didn't think he would really kill me physically, but I knew he would make me so weak that I would start to disappear. I didn't write those letters."

"I know."

"I just wanted to live my life. Without him. With my kids." The smile returned. "They're so great. Tough and sweet and determined. They don't care about the surgeries or the recoveries. They never complain about the pain. They just want to be normal. I could do that. Oh, not me personally. Doctors perform the real miracles. But I could help. I could pull it all together. And the more I worked with those kids, the stronger I got."

Her words shamed him. She was everything she claimed, and he'd been too caught up in his own pain to notice. He'd abused his position in her life to bully her. In his own way, he was no better than Hilliard.

"Why do you talk about being strong and weak?" he asked.

"Because I have to stay strong. I have to make life better. I never wanted to be useless or frail or crazy."

"You're not crazy."

Her eyes had dilated so much, they were black instead of blue. She blinked. "It's there, you know. The fear of it. Lurking. Breathing like a great beast. It calls to me, but I turn my back on the sounds. I ignore the whispers."

"What whispers?"

"The ones that say I'm like my mother. That I'm crazy, too."

He knew he shouldn't ask. That it wasn't his damn business. But he wanted to know.

"Your mother's been gone for a long time. What does she have to do with anything?"

"She was weak," Madison whispered. "Crazy. She would go away for long periods of time. They always told me she was resting. When I was little I used to wonder why my mother was always so tired, but as I got older I realized they were just keeping the truth from me. She was locked away in a mental institution."

"You don't have to tell me this," Tanner said, sorry he'd asked. Not because he didn't want to know, but because it was wrong to be listening.

"She was so beautiful," Madison continued as if she hadn't heard him. "So beautiful. Everyone said she was. They said I looked like her, but I didn't. Not even close. When she was home and feeling better, she would play with me and dress me and do my hair. But when she was sick…"

Madison curled her fingers into her palm. "I learned to stay away from her then. She was so quiet, so still, that she scared me. It was as if she were trying to disappear. And then she would go away." She stared at her lap. "In the end, she was the happiest I'd ever seen her. That's what made it so horrible. She was happy. We went to a movie together. We'd never done that. The doctors were hopeful, my father talked about us taking a vacation. Then I came home from school one afternoon and there was blood everywhere. They tried to keep me from seeing it, but I saw it anyway. She was gone. I always thought that was why she'd been so happy. She'd finally decided what she should do."

"Madison, stop."

She looked at him. "Christopher used to say I was like her. That I was weak and eventually I would take my own life. I said that wasn't true, but sometimes I wondered if it was. Sometimes I was afraid of what I would become."

He stood and pulled her to her feet. She had trouble maintaining her balance, so he drew her close and wrapped his arms around her.

"I'm sorry," he whispered into her hair. "Sorry for doing this to you. I should have believed you."

"You were angry," she said. "You're not so angry now."

He bent over and scooped her up in his arms. She relaxed into his embrace, as trusting as a child.

She didn't say anything on the short journey back to her room. He placed her on the bed and smoothed her hair out of her face.

"You should sleep now," he told her. "Try to rest. In a couple of hours, the drug will have worn off and you'll feel better."

Before he could move away, she grabbed his hand to hold him in place.

"I wish it had been me," she told him. "Instead of your friend. I wish it had been me."

Still in the grip of the strong drug he'd given her, he knew she spoke the truth. He would have known it anyway.

"You don't have to wish that," he said.

"I know, but I do."

She released his hand and closed her eyes. He moved to the doorway, where he watched her for several minutes. He might have rescued her and kept her safe from her ex-husband, but he hadn't earned the right to do what he'd done to her. The kicker was, all the regrets in the world didn't give him a way to take it back.

Chapter 9

Madison woke with the sense of having lost time. She couldn't explain the sensation any more clearly than that. It was dark outside, so she knew she'd missed most of the afternoon, but she had no recollection of hours passing or of having slept. It was as if her memory had developed a black hole.

She sat up and silently tested herself with a series of questions. Yes, she knew who she was and where she was. The reasons for her being there made sense and she knew the name of the current president. So why did she have a nagging sense of something being wrong?

There wasn't any answer. She slowly stood, wobbling only a little. Had she been—

Memory returned. Not much, just the hint of an argument with Tanner. Something about him being angry and her not wanting to take the truth drug. She didn't re-call everything that had happened, but she didn't like it. Worse, she couldn't remember what she'd said to him.

She reached up and rubbed her head, as if she could find what was missing. She had the sense of being…vi-olated. Not physically, she thought. But in her mind.

"Not possible," she whispered. Except she couldn't shake the belief that it was.

She left her room and started down the hall. Tanner sat in the kitchen, a cup of coffee in front of him. When he heard her, he looked up.

"How are you feeling?"

A simple question, she thought. Nothing upsetting about that. Yet for the first time since she'd met him, she felt afraid. Not so much of him, but in general.

"I can't remember anything about what happened," she said.

"That's what happens. It will wear off."

"Will my memory return?"

"No."

So the void would linger, and she would always won-der what happened and what she said.

"You need to eat," he told her. "That will help get the chemicals out of your system."

Chemicals he had put there.

She searched his face, looking for hints or clues as to what had happened. There weren't either, but there was something….

"I'll fix you some soup," he said. "Toast. You don't want anything heavy."

He made the statement without looking at her, without meeting her gaze. If he were anyone else, she would say he felt guilty.

"What did you do to me?" she asked. "Why am I afraid of you?"

He stood and faced her. Once again he wore all black. The dark, dangerous man who knew how to kill. She took a step back.

"You're reacting to the drug. It will make you anxious for a few days."

"No. This is about you." She forced herself to breathe slowly. To think logically. What had happened? "Did you find out what you needed to?"

He nodded.

"Did you ask more than you should have?"

"You told me more."

She forced herself to stand in place when she really wanted to step back and move away from him. What had she said? What secrets had she shared?

"Did you try to stop me?" she asked.

He turned toward the stove. "Go out onto the patio. I'll bring you something to eat."

She wanted to run out of this house and never see him again. The dull gleam of the security bracelet she wore reminded her that she was truly trapped here. There would be no running without Tanner's permission.

Tanner fixed soup and toast, as he'd promised. He put both on a tray, along with some tea, and carried them outside.

Madison sat in the dark at the patio table. Although

there were lights and switches by the slider, she hadn't bothered to turn them on. The sun had only set an hour or so ago, so the air was still warm. Crickets called out from the edges of the garden.

She didn't glance at him or acknowledge his presence. He felt her disapproval and his own guilt.

"I'm sorry," he said as he set down the tray in front of her. "I was angry about Kelly and I took it out on you."

"I trusted you."

"I know."

"You betrayed that."

She couldn't know for sure, but she was right. He *had* betrayed her.

"Yes." He pushed the tray toward her. "You need to eat. You'll feel better afterward."

"I should listen to you why?"

"Because I'm all you have right now."

She finally looked at him. Even in the darkness he could see the hurt in her expression. "Gee, what does that say about my life?"

"Madison…"

"Go away."

He probably should have, but he couldn't. Instead he took the seat across from her and leaned back in the chair. "You maybe have noticed I have this thing against rich women," he said.

"Not really."

He looked at her. "Now I know you're lying."

She shrugged, then reached for the tea. "Whatever."

"There's a good reason."

"Good, maybe. Interesting? Unlikely."

She wanted to wound him. Payback, he thought, knowing he'd earned it.

"I grew up in the barrio of Los Angeles," he said. "About fifteen miles from here. The only mostly Anglo kid on my street or in my class. My mother died of a drug overdose when I was five and I never knew my father. My grandmother raised me. She was tiny, religious and lived her life in fear of me losing my immortal soul."

He smiled as he thought about the amazing woman who had raised him. "She couldn't stop me from joining a gang when I turned twelve or getting arrested more times than either of us could count. By the time I turned eighteen, I'd spent a total of three years in juvenile detention and jail. I didn't expect to make it to my twenty-fifth birthday. I'm not sure she did, either. Gang life was hard and dangerous. But she was determined I would be one of the rare ones who made it out. She insisted I go to mass with her twice a week, if I wasn't locked up, and she never stopped praying for my soul. She wanted more for me."

Madison started on her soup without speaking. Tanner told himself that silence was a good sign. He didn't usually talk about his past with anyone, but he knew he owed her something and this was all he could think of.

"She begged me to give up the gang, to find another goal. Something that would give me a future. Two weeks before my eighteenth birthday, Nana was fatally shot in a drive-by shooting. She'd been in the wrong place at the wrong time. I couldn't even go after someone for revenge—the shooter was in my own gang."

Madison raised her gaze to his. "Was it you?"

"No. I wasn't around when it happened or I would have prevented it. Instead I could only hold her hand as she slowly bled to death."

"I'm sorry."

"Me, too. She was…" He hesitated, then figured he might as well say it all. "She's the only person I've ever really loved and the only one who loved me back. I told her I would make things right, but I didn't know how. You can't kill someone in your own gang, although I was willing to for her. She told me to forget about the gang and the streets. To leave. She made me promise to join the Marines for one tour. That was all. When that was done, I could do whatever I wanted with my life. So I agreed. I buried her and enlisted on the same day."

"Things seem to have worked out the way she wanted."

"Yeah. I got out of the inner city, saw some of the world. Grew up. Once I realized I'd been damn lucky to escape with my life, I never wanted to go back."

"Good for you."

He shrugged. "Good for her. For never giving up. After life on the streets, life in the service was a snap. When my tour ended, I found work as a mercenary. I took to it."

"I can imagine."

"I worked my way into a job with a high-profile security company. Long hours, great pay and I got to see the world."

She picked up the toast. "There's a woman involved, isn't there?"

"Oh, yeah."

"Rich?"

"Kidnapped daughter of a Swiss banker."

"Ah. Let me guess. You rescued her and at the same time swept her off her feet with your many charms."

Despite the tension between them, he smiled. "Pretty much."

"Really?"

"Are you surprised because you don't think I'm charming or because it's such a cliché?"

Madison considered the question. "Both."

"She was young and spoiled and enjoyed being rescued. I became her flavor of the month. For reasons not clear to anyone, she wanted to marry me. Her father didn't approve but he wasn't used to telling her no."

"You said you hadn't loved anyone but your grandmother. So you didn't love her?"

"I thought I did. We set up housekeeping in Paris. I worked European jobs and she went back to her life. Neither of us was especially good at marriage. I realized she'd grown tired of our arrangement when I came home and found her in bed with a Greek shipping tycoon. I could handle the infidelity. It was being a part of a second cliché that did us in."

"So you come by your dislike of wealthy women honestly."

"In a way."

Madison finished the toast. As Tanner had promised, she felt better than she had. At least physically. Emotionally she was still shaky.

He was trying. She could see proof of that. He felt badly for what he'd done. But that didn't erase the act.

She felt violated—as if he'd assaulted her. Not physically, but in her mind. In a way, that was worse.

Hearing about his past made him more human. She liked knowing he had frailties like everyone else. But it wasn't enough.

"With power comes responsibility," she told him.

His dark gaze sharpened. "I agree."

"You blew it big-time."

"Yes."

"You manhandled me and you drugged me."

She waited, wondering if he would use the excuse that she'd agreed to the truth serum as a way to prove her innocence. Funny how that seemed a lifetime ago.

"I can't justify what I did," he said quietly. "I can only apologize and offer to have someone else come stay here with you."

"What do you mean?"

"One of my other men. I have a team. My second in command is very capable. He could stay here while I work the problem from another location. I would continue the investigation of Hilliard, but you wouldn't have to deal with me directly."

She hadn't expected that. Emotions swirled inside of her and she wasn't sure what they meant. Her overriding urge was to beg him to stay. She didn't want to start over with someone else.

"Why would you do that?" she asked.

"Because you aren't comfortable around me. I don't want to make you feel worse."

"I thought you didn't care about me. I thought I was a drama queen."

One shoulder raised slightly. "That was before I knew you."

Which meant what? That he felt differently now? That she mattered?

"I want you to protect my father," she said. "I don't care if there's reason to or not. I want someone around to make sure Christopher doesn't try anything."

"Agreed."

Just like that. She studied Tanner more closely. There were shadows she hadn't seen before. An odd set to his mouth. When he'd drugged her, she'd felt his anger as if it were her own. Now she felt his guilt, remorse and shame. Christopher had never felt anything but satisfaction when he'd hurt her.

"If you could take it back—" she began.

"I'd do everything differently," he told her. "I've never done anything like that before." He grimaced. "There's a guy's line. In this case it's true. I hate what I did to you. There's no excuse for it."

She believed him. Maybe it was dumb or risky, but she did. Still, she had to know what had happened.

"What did we talk about?"

He hesitated before answering. "Your mother."

Madison hadn't expected that. "I told you she was crazy?"

"You told me about her going away for rests and how she wanted to disappear. You said you were afraid of being like her and that in the end, she killed herself."

All her secrets, she thought sadly. Laid bare for him to pick over and judge.

"You couldn't just ask me about my sex life?" she

said with a lightness she didn't feel. Embarrassment gripped her, making her want to squirm.

He reached across the table and took her hand in his. Strong fingers held hers, offering comfort. She surprised herself by accepting it. After all that had happened, she would have thought she would still be physically afraid of him. Apparently not.

"You're not crazy," he said, staring into her eyes. "You're sane and rational. More than that, you're strong. You were kidnapped by your ex-husband and held for twelve days. You didn't crack. Not even close. When I came and got you, you managed to convince me to help you, and I'm not an easy sell. You're made of steel, Madison. Whatever happens, he's not going to break you. I think he knows that and it scares the hell out of him."

She didn't know what to say. Oddly enough, she wanted to burst into tears, throw herself at Tanner and have him hold her tight.

She didn't do any of it. "You sure know how to turn a girl's head."

"I mean it. I respect you."

Coming from him, that was high praise. "I appreciate that. I…" She pulled her hand free of his and dropped it to her lap. "I know why you did it," she said in a low voice. "You were angry about Kelly's death. You wanted someone punished and I was close."

"It wasn't your fault. Madison, you're the innocent in all this. You didn't ask to be kidnapped and you sure didn't do anything to make things go wrong. If anyone's to blame, it's me. I'm the one who sent him on the assignment."

He drew in a deep breath. "You're right. I was angry. Beyond angry. He was a great kid with his whole life in front of him. I lashed out and you were convenient." He turned away and stared out into the night. "I've never let feelings get in the way before. I can't tell you how much I regret my actions."

The night was still, as if the crickets had stopped their songs just to listen.

"I know." She believed him because she felt his pain. Because she believed he was basically a good man who had been pushed too far, unlike Christopher, who had never believed he'd done anything wrong.

"Thank you," Tanner murmured.

Now it was her turn to reach out. She touched his upper arm, just above the sleeve seam on his T-shirt. "Has it occurred to you that neither of us is to blame for Kelly's death?" she asked. "Doesn't that lie with the person who pulled the trigger and Christopher, who hired him in the first place?"

"Good point."

She didn't think she'd actually convinced him that it wasn't his fault, but maybe he could consider the possibility. Bad enough to mourn the death of a friend without the added burden of being the reason he was gone.

"You don't need to leave," she said.

Tanner stared at her. "Are you sure? I can have someone else here within the hour."

"Any plans to drug me again?" she asked.

"Don't joke about that."

"I'm not."

"Then no. I'll never do that again."

Something had shifted between them. She couldn't explain it and she wasn't sure she even understood it. Maybe it was his guilt or his attempts to level the playing field by sharing his past with her. Maybe it was that she believed he thought she was strong. Maybe it was that they'd both been rubbed raw emotionally and that had brought them together. In some strange way, she felt as if she knew Tanner better than she'd known anyone in her life.

"You can stay," she told him and meant it.

Chapter 10

Madison was surprised by how good she felt the next morning. She woke up feeling energetic and actually hopeful about her situation. Maybe it was knowing that Tanner was firmly on her side. She wouldn't want him as an enemy, but as a member of her team, he was invaluable.

She showered and dressed, then left her bedroom. The scent of coffee drew her to the kitchen. The pot was full and there was a bowl of fresh blueberries on the counter. After pouring herself a mug of coffee and grabbing a handful of berries, she wandered toward the control room.

She felt both compelled to see Tanner and nervous about seeing him. The odd combination made her hover outside without saying anything.

He sat at his computer. There was no way to tell how

long he'd been at it, but he struck her as an early riser. From this angle, she had a clear view of his profile— all sharp angles and strong jaw. Thick muscles pulled at the sleeves of his T-shirt. His hair was short but thick. His mouth firm and unsmiling. There was nothing soft about him, nothing that yielded.

"How long are you going to stand there?" he asked without looking up from the screen.

"I'm not sure. Maybe five more minutes."

He turned to her and offered a faint smile. "Or you could come in and pull up a chair."

She raised her eyebrows. "What about the security system? Won't I be instructed to return to my authorized perimeter?"

"I've cleared you for the entire house. You'll only set off an alarm if you go outside."

"Really?" The man never ceased to surprise her. "Why?"

"Because I trust you."

The words shouldn't have mattered, but they did. She knew he still felt badly about what he'd done the previous day. Guilt wasn't a big deal—it didn't change the facts. But trust was different. Tanner was not a man who gave that easily.

She walked into the control room. Sure enough, the security computer remained silent on the subject. Tanner grabbed a chair and pulled it close to his.

"Want to see what I'm doing?" he asked.

"Sure."

She settled next to him and held out her hand. "Want some?"

"Thanks." He took a couple of berries, then popped them in his mouth. "I've been receiving reports from the people I have following Hilliard. We're tracking his movements, learning his patterns, tapping his phone calls."

She glanced at Tanner as she ate the rest of the berries. "That's illegal."

"Yeah, gee, it is. Huh. I guess that makes me a really bad citizen."

"Okay. Point taken. It's something you need to do to find out what he's up to. Anything?"

"No. He has a secure line we're not able to tap into. Same with his computer. I know when he's online, but I can't get into his system."

"Has he met with anyone interesting?"

"A few. Several men came to see him yesterday. I don't know who they are yet, but I will. According to my guy, Hilliard was pretty shaken after the meeting. He's up to his neck in trouble, I just don't know what kind. But I will. There's cereal and milk, or I could make pancakes."

The sudden switch in topic caught her off guard. "What? Oh. Breakfast. I'm okay. My stomach is still a little queasy."

"You need to eat. You're too skinny."

"Mr. Keane, you certainly know how to turn a woman's head."

"You know I'm right. You're like a twig. Get some meat on those bones."

She wasn't actually offended by his brusque comments. She knew he meant them for her own good, but she liked the idea of teasing him.

"Again I bask in the glow of your warm words."

He glared at her. "I'm serious."

"So am I."

He sighed heavily. "You have to know you're beautiful, Madison. That's not what this is about. You've been in a stressful situation for nearly two weeks. My screwup yesterday didn't help. You haven't been eating or sleeping. It's going to take a while for you to build up your reserves. As it is, your immune system is compromised and you've probably lost significant muscle tone. You have to counter that by eating healthy, getting rest and exercise. There's a gym in the back bedroom. Feel free to use it whenever you want. In the meantime, eat some damn breakfast."

The last words were practically a shout. She didn't know what to say or think. Okay, there had been a lot of information in that little speech of his, but the only thing she could focus on was that he thought she was beautiful.

Without meaning to, she touched her left cheek, fingering the scar there. He grabbed her hand and pulled it away.

"The scar doesn't matter," he said.

"That's not what Christopher said. He hated that I wouldn't get it fixed."

She waited for him to ask why she hadn't. But Tanner was nothing like her ex. Instead he smiled at her.

"The scar doesn't matter," he repeated.

In that moment, she believed him.

Quiet settled between them. She found herself getting lost in his dark eyes, searching them for emotion and secrets. Before, she would have only accused him of the latter, but now she knew better. Tanner cared. It took a while to uncover the feelings, but they were there.

She suddenly realized he still held her hand. Somehow his fingers were tangled in hers and it felt…right.

Whoa—talk about a place she wasn't going to go. She pulled back her hand and rose. "Okay, I'm going to go get something to eat. Do you want anything?"

"No, thanks."

She took her coffee and left. In the kitchen she made herself an egg and toast. As she ate, she wondered what was going on inside her brain. Why was she attracted to Tanner? Was it the situation—a victim wildly grateful to her rescuer? Was it that everything was so raw between them, so there wasn't time or energy for games? Was it the man himself?

Did it matter?

Nothing was going to happen. That wasn't what this was about. Plus, after Christopher, she'd given up on men. They couldn't be trusted.

She finished her breakfast, then cleared the dishes. How ironic that she'd decided to live without a relationship in her life because she couldn't trust men, yet she trusted Tanner with her life. She felt as if yesterday had shown her the worst he had to offer and she'd survived. That she could take him on and win. Probably not in hand-to-hand combat, she thought with a smile, but elsewhere.

She returned to her room, where she went to work on her laptop. There wasn't much she could do from a remote location. She'd already turned over all her open cases to another staff member, but she could certainly keep in touch with her former clients and their families.

An hour later, Tanner knocked on the open door. "Got a minute?" he asked.

"Sure." She put her computer into sleep mode and slid off the bed. "What's going on?"

"Hilliard takes a laptop to and from the office. It's a daily thing and he never misses." He led the way back to the control room. "Know anything about it?"

"It's something he's always done. He downloads sensitive information into his laptop and keeps it close. The computer itself is special. He got a new one every year—faster with better encryption."

Tanner grimaced. "Figures the guy would get fancy. Where does he keep it in the house?"

"There's a safe in his office."

"Do you know where?"

She smiled. "Of course."

They sat down at the desk and he handed her a pad of paper. She quickly sketched the downstairs floor plan. "There's a built-in bookcase and storage unit against this wall," she said, pointing to her drawing. "The left cabinet holds the safe."

"You wouldn't happen to know what kind?" he asked.

"Sorry, no. But I know the combination."

"I'm going to guess that's been changed."

"Good point." She'd been gone for over a year. She doubted very much had stayed the same.

"Is the safe built into the cabinet, or does it come out?"

Madison did her best to picture what Christopher's office had looked like. "I think it's built in. I never used the safe myself. It was strictly for his papers. I wasn't supposed to know the combination, but he made such a big deal about keeping it from me that I made it a point to learn it." She shrugged. "Not very mature of me, I know. It took about six months for me to get all six numbers. Then I used to open it because I could."

Tanner grinned. "That's my girl."

"I have my moments." She pointed at the drawing. "Are you going to break in?"

"Maybe."

"Can I come?"

"No."

Why was she not surprised? "This isn't a guy thing, right? You have women on your team."

He hesitated just long enough to annoy her. She glared at him. "Dammit, Tanner, welcome to the new century. Women can do everything a man can do with the exception of peeing while standing up. Who do you think you are not having women on your team? It's misogynistic. It's disgusting. It makes me want to sock you in the arm."

He held up both hands in a gesture of surrender. "Hey, grumpy girl, before you decide to beat the crap out of me, give me a chance to answer the charge. Yes, I have women on my team, but I don't want to go into it because their lives are my responsibility and I don't discuss the details of my employees. I agree that women are just as capable as men, and if you tried to hit me, especially in the arm, you'd only hurt your hand."

As she'd felt his muscles herself, she knew that was probably the case, but she wasn't going to admit that to him.

"I'm tough," she said.

"I've already agreed to that."

"Tougher than you."

He raised his eyebrows and didn't speak.

"Okay, maybe not tougher, but *as* tough," she said.

"On a really good day, maybe. For about ten minutes."

She grinned. "Fair enough."

He smiled.

They looked at each other for a full minute. Madison felt a definite tension crackle in the air. Awareness, she thought, as heat invaded her belly and swirled out in all directions.

Tanner broke the spell by lowering his hands and turning his attention back to the drawing. "I'll see what I can come up with," he said. "I'm going to call your ex just to mess with his head. Want to listen?"

It was the perfect distraction, she thought. Tension dissolved and her attention shifted back to the matter at hand.

"Absolutely. Will he be able to hear me calling him names?"

"Not if you don't talk."

"I can be quiet."

He moved her to a desk across from his, then handed her a headset. She settled it in place while he dialed a number, then asked to be put through to Christopher Hilliard.

"Keane? What the hell kind of game are you playing?"

Christopher spoke without warning. There was no click of a receiver being picked up or subtle buzz in her headset. One second there had been silence, the next his words.

Madison felt as if she'd fallen through the ice. Her

blood went cold and she couldn't breathe. Yesterday she'd been afraid of Tanner, but that feeling had nothing to do with the terror that now swept through her body and left her immobilized. Every fiber of her being screamed at her to get away—that this man wanted to kill her. Only supreme force of will and being in a place he could never find her made it possible for her to stay in her seat and pretend calm.

"My game," Tanner said calmly. "I'm changing the rules again."

"Meaning what?"

He looked at her and winked. "Meaning I really like your wife and I'm going to keep her around a little while longer."

"You bastard."

"I want to tell you that's not true, but from what I've heard, my parents weren't married. Pity."

Christopher swore. "You can't do this." Rage sharpened every word.

"As I'm the one currently serving host to Madison, I'm going to say I can. She's staying here, Hilliard, until I say otherwise."

"I'll go to the police."

"I heard that one before. You didn't call them, though, did you? I wonder why not. Is there something you don't want them to know?"

"I'll get you for this," Christopher told him.

"First you'd have to find me, and that's not going to happen."

"Want to bet?"

"Sure." Tanner smiled. "Come and find me, Hilliard.

I'd like nothing more than a little one-on-one time with you."

"You'll be sorry you defied me."

"Good to know. While we're establishing rules, let me be clear. You come after Madison again, Hilliard, and you're dead. I'll do it myself."

"You wouldn't dare."

Tanner straightened. His expression turned serious, his body stiffened. "Try me."

Madison heard her ex's sharp intake of air before he hung up. Tanner set his phone back on the receiver and Madison pulled off the headset.

"That went well," she said, trying for a cheerfulness she didn't feel. "I'm sure you scared him."

"That was the point. I want to make him nervous. That's the quickest way to make him screw up." He looked at her. "You okay?"

"Fine. I didn't like hearing his voice, but I survived."

He stood and walked over to the desk where she sat. "We could take it off," he said, lightly touching the band around her wrist. "It's your call."

"Really?" He trusted her that much? "You're making it my choice. That means there's a reason for keeping it on."

"If the unlikely happens and he does find you and grab you, the alarm would go off. It's not only loud enough to wake the dead, it pages me wherever I am. I would know instantly."

"But he won't find us."

"No."

"But it's not impossible that he could."

"Few things are impossible."

She stared at the metal bracelet. "I'll keep it on for now."

"Okay."

Chapter 11

Tanner continued his research into Hilliard's life while asking one of his team members to check out the security system at Hilliard's house. Even if it was state-of-the-art, there was a way around it. The question was, how difficult would the break-in be? Tanner wanted a look at that computer.

Whatever the other man was up to was tied in with Madison's kidnapping. She'd said it was all about the money and he, Tanner, believed her. But why did Hilliard need so much cash? Not for his gambling debts. So what did he want to buy and from whom? If Tanner could get even one of those questions answered, he could solve the whole mystery.

In time, he told himself. He was patient and thorough. That meant he would win.

"Knock, knock." Madison stood at the entrance to the control room. "I made lunch. Chicken-salad sandwiches with an avocado-and-tomato salad. Want some?"

As a guy who frequently lived on convenience food, he didn't have to be asked twice.

"Sure. Thanks. You don't have to cook."

She nodded. "I know, but you've made the last couple of meals and I actually like cooking. As long as there's no pressure. I could never stand those fifteen-course dinners Christopher was so fond of giving. Fortunately I was only responsible for finding the caterer. He didn't want me to prepare anything myself."

Tanner followed her into the kitchen, where he washed his hands at the sink before taking a seat at the table. "Why not?"

"He didn't believe that I could."

Tanner glanced from her to the artfully arranged sandwiches, the salad made with several kinds of lettuce and an obviously homemade vinaigrette. "You're kidding."

"He didn't think I was capable of very much." She stirred the dressing, then handed it to him. "My special blend."

"So you were completely invisible to the guy," he said as he took it and sprinkled a large spoonful onto his salad.

"He preferred it that way. To him I was like the furniture. There to be of service and look good. You don't expect your sofa to have an opinion and you sure wouldn't listen if it did."

"You're not a sofa."

"I was to him."

She spoke with the acceptance of someone long used to the reality, however unpleasant.

"You got away," he pointed out.

"Yes, I did, and I'm going to stay away. I'm lucky—I was never dependent on him financially. We didn't have children, so I shouldn't have to have anything to do with him. That's my plan. A Christopher-free life."

"I'm going to make that happen."

"I appreciate it."

She bit into her sandwich and chewed. He did the same. The chicken mixture had a spice he couldn't place and the bread had been lightly toasted. Sunlight spilled into the kitchen and touched the right side of her face. With the scar in shadow, she was perfect. Even with it, she was pretty damn spectacular.

"What happens after you get rid of your ex?" he asked.

"I return to my life. Work, mostly. I have a few friends who are very supportive."

"What about kids of your own?"

She smiled. "I'd like that. I always thought I'd be a mom. Christopher wanted me to wait, and now I'm so grateful I did. I wouldn't want any child going through this."

"Is there a Mr. Madison on the horizon?"

He braced himself for the answer. She was the type of woman who had to fight men off. No doubt there were dozens waiting in the wings.

"I gave up on the whole boy-girl thing," she said to him. "Christopher was enough to cure me."

"Not forever."

"Pretty much. I now have serious trust issues.

Plus—" she leaned toward him and smiled "—I don't have to be married to have a baby."

"I know that. But it's hard to picture you living alone."

"Why?"

"You're social."

She laughed. "Maybe compared to someone like you, but to the rest of the world I'm the quiet type."

"What do you mean someone like me?"

"You're solitary. The literary lone wolf. Besides, who are you to be asking questions? I don't see a wife around here."

"Not good for business."

"Meaning?"

"I'm gone too much." There was more to it than that. "I don't want the distraction."

She shook her head. "All crap, Tanner. You have trust issues, too."

"Maybe."

"There's no maybe. It's true. But somehow I don't think that means you lack for female companionship."

He didn't want to be having this conversation. "Can we talk about something else?"

"Of course not. This is wildly interesting. So do you spell out the rules ahead of time?"

He shifted in his chair. "What rules?"

"Sex only, don't expect me to call afterward, forget my name. Those rules."

"I'm not a jerk about it."

She smiled again. "But I'm close on the rules, huh?"

"You did okay."

They ate in silence. Tanner found himself enjoying the company even when they weren't talking. Madison was restful. Damn smart, too. Had she been someone else—someone less high-profile and without so much to lose—he would have considered recruiting her. Not that she would be interested. Her world was her kids.

But he wouldn't mind her sticking around.

As soon as the thought formed, he squashed it. She was exactly what he'd been talking about a minute ago—a distraction. And distractions got a man killed.

When Madison finished with her e-mail and notes, she logged on to her favorite shopping Web site. While she had no intention of actually *buying* shoes, it never hurt to look.

She flipped through several pages before pausing to salivate over a pair of strappy sandals she had absolutely no use for.

"But they're so cute," she murmured. And a really pale green. She didn't have any shoes that color—or any clothes, which meant the possibility of having to get a new outfit to go with her shoes. Which was just plain dumb but very tempting.

She moved the cursor to the size selection, but before she could click on it, an instant message popped up in the center of her screen.

The rectangle contained exactly two words: Hello, Madison.

She scrambled off the bed and ran out of the room.

"Tanner!" she screamed. "Tanner, he found me! He found me!"

Tanner was already halfway up the hall. She barreled into him, barely able to think or breathe or believe it was real.

He grabbed her and held her. "What are you talking about? How did Hilliard find you?"

"I don't know. He's right there." She pointed back at her room.

Tanner glanced from her to the doorway. "Get in the control room and push the red button by the door. It'll activate a security alert."

His words didn't make any sense. She forced herself to breathe in and out as she tried to figure them out. When the meaning sank in, she sagged against him.

"He's on my computer."

Tanner's expression didn't change, nor did he push her away or tell her she was crazy. Instead he wrapped his arm around her shoulders and drew her against him.

"It's okay," he said quietly. "Finding you online isn't the same as finding you here."

"But he can trace my connection."

Tanner smiled. "No, he can't."

She bit her lower lip. "Swear?"

He made an X over his heart. "Come on. Let's see what he has to say."

She allowed him to lead her back to her bedroom. She hesitated at the threshold, afraid to cross into the room. It was as if Christopher was really here, that he wanted to kidnap her again.

Tanner settled a reassuring hand on her waist. She covered his fingers with hers and led the way in. The computer sat on her bed, the cursor blinking. Now there was a second message.

Madison? Are you there?

She looked at Tanner. "Should I answer him?"

"Why not? You're safe. Maybe you can make him sweat a little. Or we could play a game."

She liked the idea of that. "What kind of game?"

"One where you make him believe he has a chance of winning you over. That could work in our favor."

"Okay. Yeah, that's good." She sat on the bed and pulled the computer onto her lap. "What should I say back?"

"That you're surprised to hear from him."

She typed the sentence, then waited. Tanner settled next to her. The mattress dipped and she found herself sliding toward him. Their hips and thighs pressed together in a way that made her aware of his physical power. Right now it was very reassuring.

I'm sorry about everything that happened, Christopher typed. You must be terrified.

Madison's chest tightened. "He doesn't know," she whispered. "He has no idea that I know he kidnapped me. That lying bastard."

"Hey, I'm the only bastard here," Tanner said.

She flashed him a smile. "Only in the technical sense. In spirit, Christopher has you beat." She thought for a second, then typed, A lot of strange stuff has been happening. I don't know what to think.

That makes sense, he responded. Madison, I'm worried about you. Please come home to me.

She shuddered. "Not for the world," she said aloud.

I want to start over with you, he added.

I don't trust you, she answered, then looked at Tanner. "He'll believe that."

Sure enough, the reply came seconds later. I'm willing to do whatever I have to in order to earn your trust.

"Can I tell him to drop dead?" she asked.

"How about saying you have to think about it."

"Okay." She typed that.

"Now disconnect," he said. "Better to leave him hanging."

She was happy to do just that. When she'd shut down her system, she set the computer on the nightstand and shifted so she faced Tanner.

"How did he know I was online?" she asked.

"It's not that hard for him to track. But knowing you're using the computer is very different from knowing where you live."

"It's still creepy."

"I know."

He touched her cheek as he spoke. At the warm brush of his fingers, she realized that she'd run to him when she'd panicked and she was okay with that. More than okay.

Heat from his body seemed to spread over her skin, making her want to sway toward him. Her gaze settled on his mouth. What was Tanner like when he was with a woman? Tough? Tender? Very intent on the details?

He stood suddenly and shoved his hands into his pockets. "I want to break into his house tomorrow night."

Her brain had to bend around the quick change in subject. "Will you have all the information you need?"

"Yeah. The last of it is due in tomorrow morning. We'll have all the details on the security system, including how to defeat it."

"I'm going to go with you."

"No."

She stood. "I know the house and the room the safe is kept in and the exact location of the cabinet. I'm a logical member of the team. Plus this is my life we're talking about."

"You're an amateur and the target. You stay where it's safe. That means in this house." His gaze turned steely. "I mean it, Madison."

"It's not your decision," she said. "I'm going."

"You think you can make me?"

She refused to back away and tried to look as mean and stern as he did. "You owe me, Tanner."

Nothing about his body changed, yet she felt a subtle shift. She knew in that moment she'd won.

"I don't want you dead," he said flatly.

"I don't want that either. But I'm still going."

He shook his head as if regretting the decision. "Okay."

Chapter 12

Madison dressed all in black, per Tanner's request. She felt like an extra in a James Bond movie and did her best to focus on that rather than on the nerves currently doing yoga in her midsection. Wanting to be part of the team was one thing, but actually breaking into her ex-husband's house was another. Wasn't her entire goal to get away from Christopher?

Yet she wanted to be a part of this—mostly to prove to herself that she couldn't be defined by her fear.

"A really dumb time to want to make an emotional statement," she told herself as she quickly secured her hair in a braid.

She'd barely finished when Tanner knocked on her door.

"It's open," she called as she grabbed black shoes and walked to the bed.

He stepped inside. "Ready?"

"Just about." She slipped on one shoe and tied it, then reached for the other. "I'm feeling all stealthy and invisible."

"Good. Here." He tossed her a black baseball cap. "Your hair's like a beacon. This will cut down on the glow."

She examined the front of the cap, half expecting to see some kind of spy logo. But it was plain.

"No, we don't have a mascot," Tanner said dryly.

She grinned. "You should think about getting one. Maybe a black cat or a bat."

"Why a bat?"

"It's dark and a creature of the night."

"We're not vampires."

"Good to know."

He stared at her. "I thought you'd be nervous."

"Oh, I am. I'm hiding it with humor. Pretty clever, huh?"

"Brilliant. Angel should be here any second. We'll go over the plan, then load up."

"Do I get gear?"

"Some."

"Can I have a ray gun?"

Tanner sighed heavily. "How much coffee did you have today?"

It was already well after midnight. Tanner had warned her that they would plan to be at Christopher's house around two in the morning. Although she'd napped, she'd worried about not being alert enough.

"Five cups since eight tonight," she said, feeling the caffeine coursing through her veins.

"Great. You're wired."

"And ready for action." She bounced from foot to foot, as if proving it.

"When the caffeine fades, that's going to be some crash."

"I know, but I figure I'm safe through the break-in. The adrenaline will keep me going."

"Uh-huh."

He didn't look convinced, but he didn't complain so she figured she was fine.

"Come on," he said. "Let's introduce you to Angel."

"He's here?"

Just then the doorbell rang. Madison put the cap on her head and followed Tanner down the hall.

"How do you do that?" she asked. "How did you know he was right there?"

"Experience."

She figured it had to be some kind of pager or something that told him when someone approached the building, but it was still impressive.

She hovered in the hall while Tanner let in his friend. The two men stood by the front door, talking. She watched them, noting they were both tall and lean with dark hair. When Angel glanced in her direction, she had to consciously keep from taking a step back. Instead of black or brown, his eyes were gray. A metallic, otherworldly color that made her muscles tense as fight or flight kicked in.

Technically he was better looking than Tanner, but those eyes really creeped her out. She noted a scar running down the side of his neck and wondered who had tried to kill him and what had happened when he'd failed. She doubted he was alive to tell the tale.

"Madison," Tanner said, motioning her forward. "This is Angel."

She steeled herself, plastered on a happy-to-meet-you smile and walked toward the men.

"Hi. I'm Madison."

Angel looked her over with a thoroughness that made her feel naked, then offered his hand. "Nice to meet you."

They shook, then she ducked behind Tanner. Not in an obvious way, she told herself. More in a being-a-toddler-and-shy-around-strangers way.

Angel grinned. "I make the lady nervous."

"Not nervous," she protested. "With everything that's happened in the past couple of weeks, I'm a little suspicious of strangers."

"I trust Angel with my life," Tanner told her. "You can, too."

"Good to know."

She was about to say something else when she realized that Angel was probably the other man Tanner had been talking about when he'd offered to have someone else move in. Good thing she'd refused, she thought, knowing the dark, dangerous, pale-eyed stranger as host would not have made for restful nights.

"Let's get loaded up," Tanner said.

They walked into the control room, where both men put on utility belts with all kinds of gear. She recognized some things like knives and flashlights, but little else.

They'd been over the plan several times, so she felt comfortable with the theory of what they were going to do. It was the reality she was having some trouble with.

Tanner crossed to a cabinet in the corner and drew out a vest, then motioned her over.

"Are you expecting bullets to go flying?" she asked, suddenly nervous about the evening.

"No, but better to be prepared."

He held the vest out and she slipped into it. He moved in front of her and fastened it up the front. The vest was surprisingly heavy and stiff.

"I wouldn't want to go jogging in this," she said.

"We shouldn't have to."

Bulletproof anything was her first inkling that maybe she'd gotten in over her head. The second was when Tanner offered her a gun.

"I can't—" she began as she tucked her hands behind her back.

"It's not a regular gun," he said, interrupting her. "It shoots a powerful sedative that acts instantly. If anyone comes after you, aim for his gut and fire. Keep firing until he drops."

"Okay."

She held out her hand and he set the gun on her palm. It was heavy, too. He showed her the safety and the trigger, then he strapped a holster around her hips and tucked the gun into its holder. It occurred to her that if it would drop a man instantly, she could take out both

Angel and him in a matter of seconds. Apparently Tanner wasn't worried about that.

"Flashlight," he said, handing one over.

That, at least, she could handle. It clipped into the other side of the holster.

The last thing he gave her was a cell phone, which they'd already discussed.

"It's preprogrammed," he reminded her. "If something happens, get away from the action and hit Send. You'll be connected to a man named Jack. Tell him what happened. He'll be there in less than five minutes to get you."

She didn't like that part of the plan.

"You're saying something could go wrong."

He shrugged. "It's always a possibility. I would prefer you stay here. Want to change your mind about coming?"

She shook her head. "I need to do this." She wasn't sure why, but the feeling was powerful enough to overcome her fear.

She tucked the cell phone into her jeans front pocket and prayed she wouldn't have to use it. Tanner picked up a backpack. Angel already had his. Then they walked out to the garage, where the van waited.

Madison climbed in back. The box she'd arrived in was gone. Instead there were low seats and windows that looked dark enough for her to figure that while she could see out, no one could see in. Tanner and Angel went up front, with Tanner driving.

"Alarm system?" Tanner asked as he started the engine.

"Jack's on it. The system is set to deactivate as soon as we let him know we're in place. Best point of entry is the French doors off the dining room. Not much of a lock there."

Madison crossed her arms over her chest and thought about the house's dining room. She remembered the doors but not the lock. Had Christopher changed much after she'd left? Their prenuptial agreement had cut him out of all the money she'd had before they were married, so he'd insisted on keeping the house they'd bought together shortly after their wedding. She'd agreed because the thought of staying in the house had made her skin crawl.

"You know there are security guards on duty," she said. "At least, there used to be."

"We have it covered."

Thirty minutes later, they pulled up on a side street she recognized. Tanner turned off the engine while Angel spoke quietly into some kind of walkie-talkie. Less than ten seconds later, Tanner turned to her.

"We've got an all clear. Madison, you can stay here in the van."

She had already reached for the rear door handle. "Not a chance."

She heard him sigh.

The night was cloudy and silent. The infamous June gloom had appeared on schedule, bringing night and morning clouds from an encroaching marine layer. She shivered slightly in her thin long-sleeved T-shirt but didn't complain. She didn't want to give Tanner an excuse to order her to stay behind.

"Alarm down," Angel murmured.

Tanner touched her arm. "No talking from now on,"

he said. "Hand signals only. Stay close to me. If anything starts to go wrong, get out of the house and back to the van. If Angel or I aren't with you in ten seconds, use the cell phone. Walk away from the van and head south." He pointed to the left.

She nodded. "We've been over this a dozen times. I know where south is, I know how to count to ten, I know not to come back to check on you." Although she wasn't sure she could just leave him lying there if something did go wrong.

Not surprisingly, he read her mind.

"You have to get out," he told her. "If you don't, Hilliard gets his hands on you. None of us wants that."

"Okay." It would be hard to leave Tanner behind; it would be harder to be dead.

"Let's go," he said and led the way.

They approached the house through the neighbor's yard, using a small gate she'd told Tanner about. Once in Christopher's backyard, they crouched in the bushes until the security guard walked by and turned the corner. Tanner motioned for them to go.

She'd never done anything like this before and it felt very strange and surreal to be running across the lawn of the house where she used to live. It was the middle of the night, and she was dressed in black and a bulletproof vest and armed with a gun designed to drop a man in less than two seconds. What on earth had gone wrong with her life?

Tanner crouched by the French doors. Angel moved in next to him. She had barely joined them when the doors swung open and they were inside.

She instantly saw the beauty of the plan as Angel locked the doors behind them. With the security system off, the patrolling guard would never know they were in the house. Pretty tricky, she thought with some humor before she glanced around at the room and received a jolt of déjà vu.

Everything was exactly the same. Madison stood and looked at the large inlaid wood table, the crystal vase set on the table runner. The placement, the fabric, the number of chairs at the table versus those around the edges of the room. Nothing had been moved since she'd left.

"His office," Tanner murmured.

She nodded and led the way. As they crossed in front of the living room, she noticed it was just as she remembered it. Even the flowers on the foyer table—peach roses with white orchids—were as she'd always ordered them.

Talk about creepy, she thought as they entered the den. Angel and Tanner walked to the painting behind the desk and pressed a button on the bottom of the frame. Slowly the painting moved aside. She walked up to the safe and felt her stomach sink.

"It's not the same one." Figures that was the one thing he *did* change.

Tanner looked at Angel. "We should have brought Bones."

"She's the best," Angel agreed. "Too late now."

"You can't open it?" Madison asked, trying not to panic.

"We can pick a lock," Tanner told her, "but breaking into a combination safe requires a special touch."

Great. "So do we come back later with Bones?"

Tanner grinned. "Depends. Do you care if we're not subtle?"

"No, but…"

Before she could ask what subtle had to do with it, he pulled a long cylinder from his utility belt and pointed it at the lock. There was a squirt of liquid, a horrible acrid smell, then a tiny whiff of smoke. Seconds later, what had been a very strong lock was a mass of gooey metal.

"Don't touch it," Tanner said. "It'll burn through bone."

"No kidding."

As she watched, Angel opened the safe and pulled out the laptop.

Tanner had already pulled off his backpack and unzipped it.

"Got it," he said as he slid the machine inside.

Madison raised on tiptoes to see over Angel. "Any of my jewelry in there? I'm missing a pair of diamond earrings that belonged to my grandmother."

Angel glanced at Tanner, who nodded. Angel reached into the safe and pushed aside papers until he found a small velvet box. He handed it to her.

She flipped open the lid and saw the earrings in question. "Cool. He told me he didn't have them and that I must have misplaced them. What a jerk."

"You do realize this means he'll know you were part of the break-in," Tanner said. "We're leaving behind cash and securities."

"We could take them, too. Just to throw him off our scent."

"He's not going to have any doubts. But if you want the money, feel free."

She shook her head. She wasn't interested in anything from Christopher except what belonged to her.

"These are fine," she said as she tucked the box into the pocket without the cell phone.

Tanner shrugged on the backpack. "Let's go." He led the way out.

Madison stepped back to let him go first. As she did so, she nudged the painting, which began to move back in place. Her breath caught. Angel and Tanner both moved toward the frame, but it was too late. It bumped the open safe so that the door swung closed.

There was a second of silence, followed by an ear-splitting siren as the lack of locking mechanism engaged the system.

Tanner yelled something, but she couldn't hear what over the noise. He grabbed her arm and hauled her out of the study. Lights went on upstairs.

Horror swept through her. She didn't want to be caught and she didn't want anything to happen to Tanner or Angel. How could she have been so stupid?

There weren't any answers, just a mad dash to the front door. Angel got there first and jerked it open. Instead of running toward the van, he took off around the corner. Tanner continued to drag her along.

The noise of the alarm echoed up and down the street. Lights came on in nearly every house. As they approached the van, Tanner pulled out a remote and hit it. Doors flew open and the engine started.

"Get in back," he yelled over the noise.

She nodded and dived for the safety of the van. Once she was inside, she stared out the window. The guard came from the rear of the house. He ran across the lawn, then suddenly collapsed. Angel appeared from behind a bush and ran parallel to the van.

Tanner shifted into gear and raced around the corner. As they turned, she looked back and saw Christopher bolt out of the house. She could see him yelling but couldn't hear the words over the alarm.

As they rounded the corner, Tanner leaned over and opened the door. Angel jumped inside and they sped off.

Chapter 13

They drove back in silence. When they reached the safe house, Angel disappeared without saying anything. Madison followed Tanner inside and waited for him to yell at her.

She felt horrible. Okay, yes, bumping the painting had been an accident, but it could have gotten them all killed, or caught. In her case, they were one and the same.

Once in the control room, he took the equipment from her without saying a word. She slipped out of her vest and handed him the phone. Tension radiated from him and she wondered how mad he was.

He put the vest away, then grabbed the security bracelet from the desk and held it out to her.

"Your call," he said.

She put it on, snapped it closed and waited.

But there wasn't anything else. No accusations, no screaming, nothing. Just the awful silence that made her feel small and stupid. Finally she couldn't take it anymore.

She put her hands on her hips and glared at him. "Okay, so I screwed up. Just yell at me and get it over with, will you?"

He sat in front of his computer and booted the system. "I'm not going to yell. You didn't do anything wrong."

"I bumped the painting."

"Not your fault. It could have happened to anyone."

But it hadn't. It had happened to her.

"I know you're mad," she said.

"I'm fine."

"You're lying."

"Madison, I promise you I'm not angry with you. We have what we needed and we all got out safely. That's what matters."

He returned his attention to the computer, which just made her want to throw something.

What was going on? He was obviously in a temper.

"Dammit, Tanner, don't do this. Don't shut me out like I'm some kid and don't treat me like I'm an idiot. You're not fine, you're furious."

He stared at the computer for several seconds before springing to his feet and glaring at her. "You do *not* want to have this conversation with me."

"Of course I do. I can handle it." At least, she was pretty sure she could.

"No, you can't." He turned and walked to the window. "Go to bed."

He couldn't have hurt her more if he'd slapped her. Just like that, she thought. One screwup and she didn't matter anymore.

"You have some pretty strict rules," she said bitterly. "You should have spelled them out before so I would have been prepared. One mistake and you're cut off. Who knew? It's amazing you have any friends at all."

She saw the tension in his body and waited for him to deny her words. When he didn't, she felt as if she had just lost something important.

"It's not that," he said quietly just as she'd turned to leave.

"Then what is it?"

"It's me."

She'd expected a lot of possible responses, but that wasn't one of them.

"How is it you?" she asked.

"I made a fundamental error in judgment and I know better. I could have gotten us all killed tonight just because I wanted to impress you."

"W-what?"

He shrugged. "Taking you was stupid. Worse. But you wanted to go and I thought…" He swore. "I thought you'd get a kick out of seeing what I did. I thought you'd be impressed by my moves. I wanted to impress you."

He turned and faced her. "I'm sorry."

She didn't know what to say, what to think. Why on earth would he care what she thought of him? Why would it matter?

"You don't even like me," she told him.

He shoved his hands in his pockets. "That's not true."

She took a step toward him. "You can't like me. Maybe you don't hate me or think I'm useless, but like? Not possible."

He sighed. "Do we have to talk about this?"

"Oh, yeah." Him liking her was cause for a serious shift in the space-time continuum. Her worry faded and something very close to happiness took its place. "We're going to talk until I understand when you hit your head."

"Why are you surprised?" he asked.

"Because I am." She moved a little closer. "How much do you like me?"

"Enough."

"How much is enough? A lot? More than ice cream?"

One corner of his mouth turned up. "Yeah. More than ice cream."

"More than a ray gun?"

"I don't have a ray gun."

"But if you could get one. If you could get the only ray gun in the universe, would you like me more than that?"

He considered the question, then shook his head. "No. Not more than that."

Maybe she was supposed to be serious, but she couldn't help laughing. "So I fall between ice cream and a ray gun?"

"Pretty much."

She could live with that.

She stood close enough that she could see the rise and fall of his chest. It was late, but she wasn't sleepy. At that moment she would swear that she might never sleep again. Awareness crackled between them. Awareness and a need that startled her with both its presence and its intensity.

She wanted him to kiss her. She wanted him to kiss her and hold her and touch her everywhere.

He stiffened. "Don't do that."

"What?"

"Don't think that way about me."

"Because you set the rules?"

"Because of what I did. Before."

Of course. He'd acted out of anger. He'd done something wrong and now he felt he didn't deserve a second chance.

As always, his expression was tough to read. There was a sharpness that was new, a tension. If she had to guess, she would swear he was more than a little interested in her—that *like* didn't begin to describe what he felt. That maybe, just maybe, he wanted her as much as she wanted him. But he wouldn't act on it. He wouldn't let himself.

She'd never pursued a man before. In her world, they came to her. There hadn't been anyone since Christopher. She simply hadn't been interested. But she was interested now.

"Tanner?"

"Not a good idea," he said flatly, although he didn't move away.

"Why not?"

"You're reacting to the situation, not to me."

Possibly. "Is that a bad thing?"

"It could be."

But for which of them? she wondered.

His eyes captivated her. The darkness seemed to pull her in. His body called to her—all hard planes and thick muscles. Did any part of him yield? Did he ever relax? And what did he look like when he slept? Suddenly she had to know.

"Tanner," she said again, this time on a breath, just as she placed her hands on his shoulders, raised herself on tiptoe and pressed her lips to his.

His mouth was firm and unresponsive. He didn't move, didn't speak, didn't blink. She lowered herself to the floor and stared at him.

"You're not going to make this easy, are you?" she asked.

"I'm not going to do this at all."

"Because I'm a client or because you don't want me?"

"Because it's not a good idea."

She had to gather her courage to say, "But you do want me."

His expression turned wry. "I'm breathing, aren't I?"

Whew. Okay, then. Now they were making progress. "Then react a little." She grabbed him by his upper arms and tried to shake him. Of course he didn't move.

"I don't want to hurt you," he said. "I don't want you to regret any—"

She reached up and covered his mouth with her fingers. "I don't have any regrets. I want this. I want you. Just for a few minutes, I want to forget everything that's happening. Please."

She felt the battle of wills within him. Would the man win or the warrior?

She waited until the tension in the room made it difficult to breathe. Finally, when she decided it was going to be a long, lonely night, he tucked a loose strand of hair behind her ear.

"I can't resist you," he said simply. Then he bent down and kissed her.

What a difference cooperation makes, she thought in delight as he wrapped his arms around her and pulled her close. This time his mouth was all giving, still firm but pressing against hers in a way designed to make her go weak at the knees. He hauled her against him so that she felt the hardness of his chest, his belly and his arousal. With one hand he pulled the elastic from the bottom of her braid and began to finger-comb her hair.

"Madison," he breathed against her mouth. "You have no idea what you do to me."

True enough, she thought hazily, enjoying the light kisses he brushed on her cheeks, her nose, her forehead before he returned to her mouth. He moved back and forth, exploring her. He sucked on her lower lip, which created fire deep inside. Her breasts ached, her thighs felt hot, her body burned for him.

When he tilted his head to deepen the kiss, she parted for him. He swept inside with a hunger that made her toes curl. He tasted of mint and coffee and of the man himself. Dark and sensual images invaded her brain. She clung to him, her fingers digging into the hard muscles of his back.

More, she thought with a desperation she'd never felt before. She needed more. More touching, more close-ness, more everything. She wanted him naked, claiming her, watching her as he thrust deeply inside of her. She wanted him trembling with need and weak in the aftermath of his pleasure. She wanted to rock his world.

He finished with her braid and moved his hands to her back. He stroked her spine, then moved lower to her rear, where he cupped the curves and squeezed. Instinctively she arched forward, which brought her belly up against his erection again. She liked what he offered and continued to rub, wanting more contact and less clothes.

He broke the kiss and nibbled along her jaw. When he reached her ear, he whispered, "My room."

"I thought you'd never ask."

Still kissing and licking the sensitive skin under her ear, he nudged her backward until they were out of the control room and moving down the hall. Anticipation tightened her belly.

When they reached his room, he released her long enough to turn on the bedside lamp. Then he cupped her face in his hands and stared into her eyes.

"I want you to be sure," he said. "I'll stop if you want me to."

As if, she thought, feeling the wetness and swelling between her legs. "No means no?" she asked.

He nodded.

"Then how about letting yes mean yes?" She pressed her hands against his chest. "Yes. I want this. I want you."

"You're sure?"

She groaned. "Jeez, Tanner, shut up and get naked. Okay?"

He chuckled. "Yes, ma'am."

He was true to his word and very speedy. In the time it took her to kick off her shoes and pull off her socks, he'd removed his boots, socks and shirt and was already working on his trousers. She decided to leave the rest of her clothes in place and instead enjoy the show.

He looked as good bare chested as he had with clothes. Powerful muscles moved and stretched in the most intriguing way. There were scars on his arms, one on his side. Later, she thought as she watched him push down his trousers and briefs in one easy movement. Later she would ask about the scars and how he'd gotten them. For now, there was the man and his very impressive arousal.

"All that for me?" she asked.

"Did you bring a friend?"

"No."

"Then it's all for you."

"Good to know."

He reached for the hem of her T-shirt. She raised her arms so he could pull it over her head, then at the last minute, dropped them to her side.

He released her and waited. She cleared her throat.

"You said I was too skinny and I am. Bony, actually. And I have no breasts. Technically the parts are there, but they're not especially large." Christopher had always wanted her to get implants, but she'd resisted. Mostly because it was what he wanted.

He stared at her for a long time, then took her right hand and brought it to his erection. He held her fingers around his thickness.

"Does this feel like I think you're anything but beautiful?" he asked.

"Well, no, but—"

He cut her off with a quick shake of his head. "Do you think I'm faking it?"

That made her smile. "Hardly."

"Then maybe you should shut up and get naked."

She laughed. "You think?"

"Absolutely."

It seemed like a good idea. She pulled off her long-sleeved T-shirt, then unfastened her jeans. Her bra went next, then her panties. When she was naked, she started to ask him what he thought, but before she could form the words, he drew her into his arms, then tumbled them both onto the bed.

They fell in a tangle of arms and legs, with him taking most of the weight. Before she could figure out if she was squishing him or not, he was kissing her and his hands were everywhere.

He touched her breasts with his fingers, teasing her nipples until she had to cry out with pleasure. He claimed her mouth, even as his fingers strolled down her belly to the waiting damp curls below.

She touched him in return, exploring his back, his chest and his arms. She kissed him with a passion she wasn't sure she'd ever felt before. Need claimed her until she felt herself pulsing with longing.

When he slipped his hand between her thighs, she sighed in gratitude. He explored her, gently discovering her secrets. Even as his thumb circled that sensitive bundle of nerves, he slipped a finger inside of her, mimicking the act of love to follow.

The steady rhythm of his touch claimed her attention. Every nerve went on alert, every muscle tensed. When he shifted so he could lean over her chest and take a nipple in his mouth, she stopped breathing. It was too much.

The nearly two years without a man combined with the skill of the man pleasing her and her own affection for him. In a matter of seconds, she couldn't hold back. Her orgasm claimed her in a shuddering release that made her cry out, even as she felt her muscles contracting over and over again.

At last she was still. Tanner moved to her side and held her close. He stroked her hair and kissed her face while she tried to recover.

"That was quick," she said after she'd caught her breath.

"You were in some pretty serious need."

"Apparently so. It's funny because I never would have thought that before. I guess I denied the physical part of my existence because it was easier than dealing with it."

He brushed his mouth over hers. "And now?"

She smiled. "Ready for round two."

"Fair enough."

He pushed himself up onto his knees, then shifted so he was between her legs. She expected him to put on a condom then enter her, but instead he bent down and lightly licked her nipples. First one, then the other. A brief, sensuous caress. It made her toes curl.

"What are you doing?" she asked.

"Round two."

"Okay. How many rounds are there?"

"As many as you want."

With that, he lowered his mouth to her breast and gently sucked. The exquisite sensation of his swirling tongue, the feel of his lips, the heat and moisture had her grabbing the bedspread and hanging on for the ride.

He moved between her breasts until she felt aroused and restless again. She wanted more. Fortunately he read her mind and began the slow journey down her belly. Kiss by kiss he moved to the promised land, where he claimed her with his mouth.

It made what he'd done with her breasts look like an amateur act. He explored all of her with his tongue, then settled on that one spot and danced with it until she wanted to scream.

She drew back her legs and dug her heels into the mattress. She pushed and writhed and panted and begged. Need filled her, yet she didn't want to find her release. Not yet. It was too good, and if she came, he would stop.

He licked and sucked and circled and nibbled until she knew she couldn't hold back any longer. When he slowly inserted a finger inside of her, she lost control and surrendered to the pleasure. Wave after wave swept through her. She knew she screamed and she might have even blacked out for a second. God love a man into the details.

This time when he tried to move next to her, she held him in place between her legs. He was still hard and obviously ready.

"Round three," she said, pulling open the nightstand drawer. "I assume you're prepared."

Instead of answering, he reached inside and drew out a box of condoms. "Is this what you were looking for?"

"Uh-huh." With what had already happened, she was eager to have him inside. She wanted to give back a little of what he'd given her.

He slipped on the protection, then slowly began to fill her. Her body stretched to accommodate him. She ran her fingers up and down his back as he reached the end then began to withdraw.

The slow, steady rhythm of his movements had her tensing in anticipation. Need sparked, then grew. Despite the intimacy of the situation, she couldn't help smiling.

"What?" he asked.

"I think it's going to happen again. You're going to think I'm insatiable."

He bent down and kissed her. "I'm going to think you're amazing."

"Oh. I like that."

He stared into her eyes, keeping nothing from her. She saw the wanting there and the pleasure as he began to move faster and faster. She felt his body tense as he claimed her over and over. Her own senses filled with his heat, his scent, his need. They strained toward each other, clinging, thrusting, pulsing until she lost herself in the wonder of it all and he pushed one last time, only to still and call out her name.

Chapter 14

Tanner lay under the covers, Madison curled up at his side. He had one arm around her, holding her close. With his free hand, he stroked her face.

"So beautiful," he said, staring into her eyes.

She smiled. "I'm okay. Plus, you're on the good side."

The side without the scar, he thought. He shifted her until she rolled onto her back and he could see the scar, then he rose on one elbow and looked down at her.

"Still beautiful," he told her.

"Thanks."

"I'm telling the truth."

"Maybe. I don't mind that this makes me different," she said, touching the raised ridge of red skin.

"Do you need it?" he asked.

She stared at him. "Why would you ask me that?"

"Because you could eliminated by a skilled p not to. There has to be a rea

She touched his mouth with that, you'll know all my secrets.

"Is that such a bad thing?"

Her gaze locked with his. "No, it Tanner."

Her words touched him in places he sworn were dead. "I'll never betray that tru

"I have to believe that." She continued to mouth with her fingertips. "I keep the scar to ren not to be stupid."

"Christopher?" he asked, settling back next to and pulling her close.

She rested her head on his shoulder and her hand on his bare chest. "Partially him."

"You'll never make that mistake again," he told her. "You learned. You're not the same person who married him."

"You don't know that."

"Actually I do."

"Okay. Maybe." She sighed. "When I met Christopher, I was everything you thought I was when you and I met. Rich, pampered, useless. I had access to as much money as I wanted, but I didn't have to do anything for it. Life was one round of parties after another. I was popular, friendly because it was easy and pretty enough to get by. No one really expected anything from me, including myself. When I met him, he treated me like a

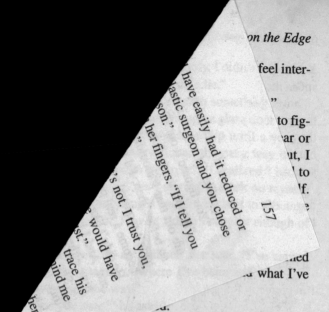

feel inter-

have easily had it reduced or
astic surgeon and you chose
son."
her fingers. "If I tell you

157

's not. I trust you.
would have
st."
trace his
ind me
her

hand back on his chest. "What do
nat I haven't earned it?"

No, that maybe you don't need the scar anymore to remember. That maybe you've learned the lesson and it's become a part of who you are."

She wrinkled her nose. "You'd like me to get the scar fixed."

He leaned close and kissed her lips. "No. I'd like you to make sure you're keeping it for yourself, not to prove something to Hilliard."

"You mean that I'm still defying him?"

"Are you?"

"Interesting point. I'll have to think about it." She snuggled closer. "Can we sleep now?"

"You want to sleep with me?"

"Sure. I— Oh." She drew back and sat up. "Right.

You're probably not the type who likes a woman to spend the night. It's okay. I'll go sleep in my own bed."

Several thoughts occurred to him at once. First, that there was an edge of pain in her voice, and he'd reached the point where he would change the tide rather than hurt her again. Second, he didn't want her to go and that scared the crap out of him.

He wrapped his arm around her and gently lowered her back to the mattress. "I would like you to stay," he said.

She shook her head. "You're just being polite."

"If that was the case, I would have said please."

"You know what I mean. You don't have to do this. I'm perfectly fine on my own."

"What if I'm not?" he asked.

She didn't look convinced. "A big, bad guy like you? What could you be scared of?"

"You're be surprised." He stroked her hair, then tucked it behind her ears. "I would really like you to sleep with me tonight."

Her gaze searched his face. As he was telling the truth, he didn't worry about what she would see there.

He knew getting too close was a bad idea. Madison didn't need the complication of a man in her life right now, and he didn't do relationships. Even if he was willing to change his rules for her, what was the point? Whatever she felt now with him was simply about the danger she'd experienced. He'd saved her and she was reacting to that. When all this was over and she returned to her normal life, she would wonder what she saw in him.

But for now she wanted to be with him, and he was willing to accept the terms. Better for both of them if this was just temporary, he told himself. Safer.

"Okay," she said with a sigh. "I'll stay."

"Great. I have to get up now."

"What?" She sat up, pulling the sheet with her, and glared at him with mock anger. "You're leaving after I've said I'll sleep with you?"

"Only for a couple of minutes." He leaned over and kissed her. "I have to set up the encryption program to start decoding Hilliard's laptop. I'm sure the program he picked is pretty tough to break into, and we can't waste any more time."

She raised her eyebrows. "Are you telling me that making love was a waste of time?"

He growled. "Stop twisting my words. You know what I meant."

"Huh. I'm not sure I do. I think when you come back to bed, you're going to have to convince me. It might take a while."

Anticipation heated his blood. "You're on."

Madison woke a little after ten and wasn't surprised to find herself alone. Even if she and Tanner hadn't gotten to sleep until almost four in the morning, he wasn't the type to stay in bed past dawn.

"Big ol' tough guy," she said with a yawn as she got out of bed and prepared to start what was left of her day.

As she showered, she stretched muscles that were mildly sore from the unaccustomed activity. Pain or not, she felt great. Whole, which was odd considering she'd never felt anything was missing.

Tanner was an interesting man. Tender in bed, which she wouldn't have expected, but still tough. He'd held her through the night. Every time she'd awakened, he'd been right there, his arms around her.

She told herself it didn't mean anything, that it couldn't mean anything—they'd only known each other a few days. Yet in some ways she felt as if she'd known Tanner forever. She'd seen him at his best and his worst. He had his flaws, but he was also a good man and she knew in her heart he would die to protect her.

Neither of them was going to die, she told herself as she stepped out of the shower. They were going to beat Christopher at his own game and win this. After that…

As she dried off, she realized she didn't know what would happen after her ex was in jail and she was free to leave. Obviously she had her job to return to, but then what? What about Tanner? Would he just walk away?

The thought made her heart ache, so she pushed it away and quickly dressed.

The smell of coffee led her to the kitchen. She passed Tanner hard at work on some strange-looking program she guessed was for encryption.

"Good morning," he said as she walked back with her mug. "I thought you'd sleep later."

"Isn't this late enough?"

"We were up late."

She thought about what they'd been doing and smiled. "Yes, we were."

He grinned. "You were great."

"So were you."

They stared at each other, still smiling foolishly, until he shooed her away.

"Back to work," he told her. "Stop distracting me."

"And how am I doing that?"

"Just by standing there."

Oh, she liked the sound of that. "So if I walked up to you and started unbuttoning my jeans…"

He shook his head. "You wouldn't even have to go that far. Just walking in would do it."

"Good to know." She gave a little wave of her fingers, then headed for her bedroom. While she wouldn't mind a repeat of last night, she thought they could both use the work time. Tonight they could focus on play.

Fifteen minutes later, she'd logged into her e-mail account and started working her way through letters from kids, along with a few notes from staff members. At the bottom of the list was an e-mail from Christopher.

Madison stared at the listed address and felt her muscles tense. Even knowing he couldn't find her, she felt unnerved by the contact. He'd just written the letter that morning—no doubt in response to the break-in.

She stood and walked toward the control room.

"I have e-mail from Christopher," she said as she entered.

Tanner looked up from a screen covered with odd symbols and lines. "What did he say?"

"I don't know. I didn't open it."

He nodded, then rolled his chair to another computer where he quickly typed on the screen. Seconds later her e-mail in-box appeared.

"Do I want to know how you did that?" she asked as she pulled up a seat for herself.

"I told you I would monitor all incoming and outgoing e-mail," he said. "The system is rigged to dump a copy in my computer. I haven't been reading it."

"As I said before, you're welcome to. Nothing very interesting."

"Until today." He scrolled down to the e-mail in question. "Want to guess what he has to say?"

She shrugged. "He's got to be furious about the break-in. Do you think he called the police?"

"Would you if you were him?"

"That depends on what I'm knee-deep in, and we still don't know that." She drew in a deep breath. "Okay— open it."

He pressed a couple of keys and the letter appeared.

Madison. I don't know what kind of a game you're playing, but that no longer matters. Your father hasn't been feeling well for days. I finally convinced him to see his doctor, who suspects a heart condition. Blaine is worried about you, which isn't helping his health. If you won't come home, at least have the compassion to contact him and put his mind at rest.

Her stomach knotted and she felt pressure in her chest. "My father," she breathed.

Tanner looked at her. "He could be lying. He's probably lying."

"But you don't know for sure."

"True, but I'm willing to take bets on it."

"Your father isn't the one who's sick."

His dark gaze sharpened. "Madison, if something was wrong with your father, the men I have watching him would have told me."

Right. "Good point. But are you sure?"

"Yes. Would you feel better if I asked them?"

She nodded. "I want to make sure he didn't go to the doctor or anything. Can they find that out?"

"They keep a complete log of his activities." He reached for a cell phone and quickly typed in a text message. "I'll hear back in less than fifteen minutes."

She drew in a breath. "Thanks. I know it's just Christopher messing with my head, but I need to be sure."

"Of course you do. He's spent your entire relationship making sure you were spooked. Why would this be any different?"

"Having you on my side helps."

"Good."

She leaned back in her chair and pointed to the computer screen with the strange symbols. "Is that the encryption program?"

"It's the antiencryption. No progress yet. Hilliard didn't use any of the better-known programs. I'm thinking he had this one custom made. Maybe somewhere in the Far East."

"Does that mean you can't break the code?"

He smiled. "It means I'll have more fun breaking it."

She looked at the lines of symbols and odd bits of text. "Are you sure?" she asked.

"Just a matter of time."

She admired his confidence and suspected he'd

earned it the hard way. Growing up in the barrio meant getting tough or getting dead.

"I know Christopher is trying to lure me out," she said. "But knowing that doesn't make me feel any better about my dad. What if he really tried something to make him sick?"

"Wouldn't Blaine notice?" he asked.

She noted he didn't say that Christopher wouldn't try something like that. Obviously if he was capable of kidnapping her, he was capable of hurting her father.

"My father is the classic absentminded professor. I don't know if he was always like that or if marrying my mother made it worse. He would often use work as an excuse to escape from her. When I was little, I used to beg him to stay, to not leave me alone with her. Not that I was scared she'd hurt me, she was just so quiet. But he never listened. He told me I would be fine and left anyway."

"That must have been hard on you."

"It was." She remembered the silence of the house and the living creature that was her fear. "As I got older, I grew less afraid of being around her. But then I worried about growing up to be like her. My father worried, too. If I laughed too loud at a party, I would catch him looking at me. If I didn't smile, if I smiled too much, he would say something. I started monitoring my own emotions, afraid I would feel too much or not enough. It was exhausting."

He leaned forward and took her hands in his. "You're not crazy. Not even close."

"I appreciate the show of support. Eventually I

gained more confidence in my own mental state to ignore the little voices in my head whispering that I was just like her."

Tanner watched the muscles in Madison's jaw tighten. Whatever she said aloud to him and the world, she still had her doubts.

"You're tough and smart and if you give in to the fear, you let Hilliard win," he said.

"I know. That's what keeps me going."

"Have you ever talked to anyone about all of this?" he asked. "A professional?"

"Therapy?" She sighed. "I saw someone before I left Christopher. She told me I was as sane as the next person and that my biggest problem was that I'd married someone emotionally and physically abusive. It helped me, but it didn't convince my father. He thinks I'm one breakdown away from turning into my mother. If Christopher got his hands on me, it would be so easy for him to lock me up. My father wouldn't do anything to stop him."

He heard the fear in her voice. "I'd stop him. Madison, I swear to you, Christopher isn't going to be allowed to put you away."

"Would you beat him up, too?"

"Would that make you feel better?"

"In the moment, but it's probably not a good idea. He'd have you arrested, and I don't think you'd like prison."

"I've been there before. I survived."

She smiled. "You were much younger then. A bad boy. I never really had a thing for the bad-boy type before."

"And now?"

"I'm starting to see the appeal."

His cell phone rang. He released her hands and reached for it. "Keane."

"Gray here, boss. You want to know if Blaine went to the doctor?"

"Hold on." Tanner plugged the cell phone into a speaker system. "Okay. I have you on speaker. Madison got an e-mail from her ex saying her father was ill. That he'd been to his doctor and was diagnosed with a heart condition."

Gray swore. "He's trying to lure her out."

Tanner looked at Madison and nodded. "That's what we think, too."

"Boss, I can tell you Blaine hasn't seen a doctor since we started watching him. He's either in his lab or he's at home. He doesn't stop anywhere on the drive back and forth. All his appointments are logged by his secretary. We've cross-checked them with the security-camera tapes we're tapping into. No one is getting in or out without us knowing about it. There haven't been any doctors in the lab." Gray chuckled. "Not any medical ones anyway. This place is crawling with Ph.D. types."

Tanner looked at Madison. "You want to ask him anything?"

She leaned toward the cell phone. "Gray, how does my father look?"

"Fine. The same. He eats the same breakfast every day while he reads the paper. His housekeeper prepares him dinner. After finishing that, he goes into his library, where he reads until he goes to bed. There haven't been any phone calls to the house."

She glanced at Tanner, then shrugged. "It's what I needed to know. My dad is fine—this is just another one of Christopher's sick games."

He nodded. "Thanks for the report, Gray. If you see or hear anything unusual, let me know right away. Hilliard is going to do whatever he can to get Madison out in the open."

"You got it, boss."

Tanner hung up the phone. "Better?"

"Yes. Thanks. You're in a very interesting business."

"Every day is different."

She smiled. "I like my days the same. Routine is very comforting."

"Soon you'll have yours back."

"Maybe." She studied her fingers, then glanced back at him. "He'll go to jail, right? He won't be free to wander the streets."

"We're going to find out what he's doing, then put him away," he told her. "For that and for the kidnapping."

"We can't prove he was the one behind it."

"We can try." He stood and pulled her to her feet, then drew her against him. "As far as I'm concerned, the job isn't over until you're safe."

She relaxed into him and wrapped her arms around his waist. "So you work for me now?"

"Yeah."

"When did that switch happen?"

"A couple of days ago."

"When are you going to let me start paying you?" she asked.

"This isn't about the money."

"You have a lot of expenses. A staff. Around-the-clock monitoring of my father. Don't worry, I can afford it."

"It's not just that," he said, trying not to smile. "There are other issues."

"Such as?"

"I don't sleep with my clients."

Her eyes widened, then her mouth curved up into a smile. "I didn't think about that. Interesting dilemma."

"Maybe we should just forget about who works for whom and go with it."

"Not a bad plan." She slid her hands around until her palms rested on his chest. "I figured we would have to wait until this evening to, um, you know."

"Having second thoughts?"

"About waiting? Absolutely. I think it's a bad idea."

Getting involved didn't make sense. Tanner knew that the more he was with her, the more he would want her. A woman like Madison only came along once in a lifetime, and that was if a man was damn lucky in the first place. If he kept this up much longer, he wouldn't want to let her go.

But there wasn't a choice, he reminded himself. She had her world and he had his. They were opposites— he lived in the shadows and she sought the light.

But now, in the twilight time between what was real and what wasn't, they could find temporary solace in each other's arms.

"What did you have in mind?" he asked.

"Well…as you're the one with the history of incarceration, I thought you might find it interesting to play escaped prisoner and the warden's wife."

He grinned. "Want to know if I have handcuffs in the cabinet?"

She laughed. "Not especially, but if you're very good, I'll let you chase me around the bed a few times."

"You're on."

Chapter 15

"It's a nice place?" Blaine asked as he sipped his glass of wine.

"Lovely. A large garden, with a view of the ocean. She has a corner room." Christopher smiled at his former father-in-law. "She's doing well."

Blaine nodded. There was an air of sadness about the old man, but resignation, too. He'd always expected his daughter to turn out like her mother. Convincing him that she had had been too easy. He should have done this years ago, Christopher thought, when he really could have locked Madison away.

"It was the kidnapping," Christopher said. "She was doing so well, but after that…" He let his words trail away and made himself think about losing everything. That should put some pain in his expression.

Blaine patted his arm. "You've been loyal to her, which is more than most men would have done. I don't know what she was thinking when she left you."

That she thought she could get away, Christopher thought. "Madison had this idea about being independent."

Blaine frowned. "She was independent enough. You never tied her down. She was free to do whatever she wanted. If only she'd known how upset you were when she left. For a while I wondered if you'd ever recover."

Christopher nodded. "It was a bad time, but not the worst. The kidnapping was the worst. As long as I live, I'll never forget that terror."

"But she's safe now. At least we have that." Blaine took another sip of his wine. "If only she'd had children. That would have grounded her."

"I wanted that, too, but Madison was afraid."

Blaine nodded. "That it would push her over the edge, like it did her mother. Maybe it's for the best."

Christopher agreed. Despite what he'd told the old man, he'd never wanted children. They were messy and got in the way. Besides, he didn't want a fat wife, and in his mind pregnancy turned a woman into a bloated gargoyle. When she'd insisted that children were important to her, he'd tried to talk Madison into using a surrogate, but she'd refused. By the end of their marriage, she hadn't wanted to discuss children at all. He'd thought that had meant she was finally coming around to his way of thinking. He hadn't known it meant she'd given up.

"How are you holding on?" Blaine asked.

"All right."

"You look tired."

"A lot of late nights in the lab."

"Are you working out those last few bugs?"

Christopher considered the question. "Getting there," he said, knowing there weren't any bugs to be worked out. The jamming device worked perfectly, it was just a matter of getting the money together to pay Stanislav the fifteen million he owed him.

"I've been thinking about what you said the other day," Blaine told him. "That we should merge our companies."

Christopher did his best to stay relaxed. He took a sip of wine, then reached for an appetizer from the tray his housekeeper had left out for them. Dinner wasn't for another twenty minutes—plenty of time for them to work out the details.

Elation filled him. If he could get the old man to agree, they could make an announcement in the morning. That would send the company stock soaring. He had half a million options he'd been holding onto. The difference would cover his next payment to Stanislav and his gambling debts.

"I'm going to be announcing the new technology in a couple of weeks," Christopher said. "It would have to be before then or not at all."

Blaine smiled at him. "You didn't tell me you were that close."

He grinned back. "I am. It's very exciting work, Blaine. I can barely tear myself away from the lab. I know it's important to run the company, but the true joy of my day comes from discovery. The trials and errors of dreaming up a design or a process, then seeing it to fruition."

"I couldn't agree more. Your parents would be very proud of you, my boy."

Christopher ducked his head, as if too modest to accept the praise. He had a feeling that if his parents could speak from the dead, they wouldn't mention much in the way of pride. Instead they would probably want to talk about the sudden failure of their brakes on that icy mountain road.

"They wanted great things for the company," he said. "I've tried to fulfill their dream, but I've missed the mark. Now, with the new technology, I'll finally be able to do what they always wanted."

"You're too hard on yourself," Blaine said. "But that's a good trait to have. It makes one work harder." He picked up his wine. "Yes, I think it's time. Let's announce the merger. We'll let the suits work out the actual details, but I want to consider this a done deal. Agreed?"

Christopher raised his glass. "Agreed."

As easy as that, he thought as he drank down the red wine. Problem solved. He would have the fifteen million for Stanislav and the five million for his gambling debts and he no longer gave a rat's ass if he ever saw Madison again.

Not that he could kill her right off. For one thing, he didn't want Blaine distracted by anything until the merger was complete. For another, he didn't know where the bitch was.

It still fried him that she'd managed to turn Keane.

Christopher had no idea how she'd done it—the man had a reputation for being ice under pressure. He was professional, seasoned and dangerous enough to make a sane man steer clear. So how had his stupid, selfish wife convinced him to not only protect her but to work for her?

He knew Keane was the one behind the break-in. Not that his laptop would do them any good. There was no way they could decrypt the hard drive. Not in a thousand years. But it annoyed Christopher that they'd dared to walk into his house to steal it along with Madison's earrings.

He wanted Madison and he wanted Keane. He had two teams of men looking for them, but so far they'd found nothing. They'd warned him Keane would disappear like smoke, and he had.

But they would find him eventually, and when they did, Christopher would lock up Madison for real. Once the merger went through, he would make sure she died in a way that made it look as if she'd taken her own life. Sad but not completely unexpected. She was, after all, her mother's daughter.

"This will work out for all of us," Blaine said. "I always worried about what would happen to my company after I was gone. I couldn't leave it to Madison—she could never handle the responsibility. With the merger, you can be in charge. That way I know she'll always be taken care of."

"You have my word," Christopher said as he rose. "Will you excuse me for a moment? I need to check on something at work."

Blaine waved him away. "I know the call of the job," he said with a smile. "But when Madison finally comes home, you're going to have to adjust your hours. She'll need you."

"I'll gladly be here for her," Christopher told him. "You know she's my world."

Blaine sighed. "I do, indeed. I felt the same way about her mother. It didn't matter that she was crazy as a loon. I loved her with all my heart."

Christopher walked out of the study and into his office. There he picked up the phone on his secure line and dialed a number he knew by heart.

"Hilliard," he said when the phone was answered. "I'll have the money for you in forty-eight hours."

"Very good," Stanislav said. "I will have the last two components. We will make our exchange at the usual place. Seven o'clock?"

"I'll be there."

"I'm sure you will be. I am pleased you have the money, Christopher. You are a man of many talents—it would be a shame to make you incapable of using them."

Madison stretched out on the sofa and stared through the open windows up at the night sky. So many night noises, she thought. The dark was never silent.

After her kidnapping experience where she was kept blindfolded for nearly two days, she would have thought she would be terrified to be out of the light. Maybe she would have been with someone else. But not with Tanner. Not only did she trust him to keep her safe but she liked how he didn't play games with her. He didn't say one thing and mean another. He didn't want to make her think she was crazy. If he was mad, he said so and acted accordingly. The rules were much simpler here.

"What are you thinking?" he asked as he brushed his fingers against her bare arm.

They were both naked beneath their robes, pleasantly sated from their evening of lovemaking. While her body rested and recovered from the pleasure it had received, her heart still wanted to be close to him.

"That you don't play games with me," she said. "You aren't trying to trick me."

"Not my style."

She smiled at him. "That would be my point. It's a good thing. Oh, and I don't think you're interested in my money."

He grimaced. "Not even a little. Besides, I have money of my own."

She grinned. "As much as me?"

"You only have a small share of Daddy's company. A few options. How much could they be worth?"

"Just ten million. Pocket change."

He groaned. "Yes, you have more money than me."

She laughed. "Don't worry about it. Besides, I don't actually have the money. I have the options, which means I'd have to cash them in to get dollars in my pocket. There's also a trust fund from my mother. That's what I live on."

"You could ask the foundation you work for to pay you."

"I could, but I won't. Why should I take a salary I don't need when that money could go toward another operation for a child?"

"Don't go all bleeding-heart do-gooder on me. I really hate that in a woman."

She wiggled her eyebrows. "Really?"

"No, not really."

"I didn't think so. But I am happy you're not interested in my money. I know Christopher was. Or at least he wanted to use me to get access to my father's company and my inheritance. The irony is, because of his name and the fortune I thought he had, it never occurred to me he would care about money. I can't even take credit for figuring it out."

"What happened?"

She snuggled closer and sighed. "It was at a party. He loved to have cocktail parties two or three times a month. Despite the fact that he accused me of doing little more than calling a caterer, they were still a lot of work for me. Although it's not as if I had an actual job or life beyond shopping and lunching with my friends." She looked at him. "This was during my useless stage."

"I doubt you were ever useless."

"Then you would be wrong. People talk about a life-changing moment. Well, this party was mine. There were all these scientists talking shop. Most of them didn't bring their wives to this country, so I was one of maybe three women, and the other two were on the team. I was circulating, playing hostess, but everyone was busy talking about computer chips and tolerances and rates of failure or whatever. I could only smile and look pretty."

"What happened?" he asked.

"I overheard Christopher with one of the scientists. The man was surprised that I didn't know anything about Christopher's work. Christopher pointed at a crystal vase on a table and said I was just like that. A beautiful, empty piece of art. He didn't expect me to think or have opinions, and fortunately for him, I'd never shown much inclination or talent at either."

Tanner kissed her forehead. "He was an idiot for not seeing there's a whole lot going on behind those big blue eyes."

"There is now, but there wasn't then. I was stunned. Humiliated. I spent the next few days thinking about what he'd said and I realized in some respects, he was right. That's when I started to make changes, to become a better person. It was a few months later that I got involved with the children's charity."

"What did the scientist say in response to Hilliard?"

She shrugged. "He was from Russia and had left his wife and children behind because his work was important and they weren't. I don't think he was shocked."

Tanner stared at her. "Russian?"

"Sure. A lot of them were. Some didn't even speak English, which made small talk a challenge. I learned a few phrases in Russian so I could chat, but Christopher told me to stop trying. That I was simply embarrassing myself and him."

"Russian?"

"Why are you repeating that?"

"Because it might be the one piece of information we've been missing. Do you remember the man's name?"

"No, but I probably have it on a guest list. I kept them on my computer so that I knew who had been invited when. I didn't want to repeat menus with the same guests."

"Can you access the information?"

"Sure."

He sat up and cupped her face. "How long after this party did Christopher start working on his new technology?"

Madison tried to remember. "It was a few months. Maybe six."

"If it were me, I wouldn't sell it all outright," he said, seeming to speak more to himself than her. "I might make him work for it. Plus, if he was fed the information a piece at a time, it would slow the process, making it appear he really had developed it himself."

"What are you saying?" she asked as he rose to his feet and drew her up beside him. "That Christopher bought his jamming device from the Russians?"

"Maybe. But the only possible seller would be the Russian Mafia. It all makes sense."

They went into the control room, where he sat her down in front of one of the computers. After pulling up the information from her hard drive, she scrolled through until she found her party file. She went through party dates, then printed out several.

"This is as close as I can get," she told Tanner. "I've narrowed it down to six."

"Don't worry. I should be able to clear most of the people as suspects right away. Then I'll focus on who's left."

"Can I help?"

"If you want to."

"Absolutely."

The quicker they figured out exactly what Christopher was up to, the quicker they could trap him. She was tired of having him screwing up her life.

"How much would something like his jamming device cost?" she asked.

"Millions. Maybe hundreds of millions."

"So he could have needed the cash from my kidnapping ransom."

"With luck, he planned on it," Tanner said. "That could put him in trouble with his seller. The Russian Mafia isn't known to be a patient creditor."

"I don't want him too desperate," she said. "That could put my father at risk."

"I know. I still have my team on him."

"Which is why I can sleep at night."

Tanner spread out the lists on the table. "Let's eliminate duplicate names. Then I'll run the list through my computer and we'll figure out who everyone is."

As she scanned the guest names, she said, "My father can't know what Christopher is doing. He's a purist. He would never approve of buying technology."

"I would guess no one knows what your ex is doing. His team may suspect, but they're unlikely to say anything."

"But wouldn't they do more than suspect?" she asked. "They would see the equipment coming in."

"I doubt it's like that. I would guess the Russians gave him a basic design and are providing a piece at a time. Hilliard takes it apart, figures out how it's put together, then recreates it over time. If the design isn't detailed, he can't jump ahead. If they're smart—and I'm guessing they are—they're holding back vital information until the very end. As far as Hilliard's company is concerned, he has a record of every step of development. He'll be able to claim the idea as his own and reap the rewards."

"You mean the billions."

"Probably."

"I hate that it's all about the money."

"Welcome to the real world." He looked up and smiled at her. "But you go on being idealistic. It's one of the things I like best about you."

"Gee, thanks. So if Christopher doesn't have my ransom money, where is he going to get the cash he needs to buy the next installment?"

"I don't know, but we should be looking for that, as well." He glanced at her. "How good are you on the Internet?"

"I can usually find shoes on sale. That's probably not very helpful."

"I'm sure we can make it work for us."

At three o'clock the next afternoon, Madison got the answer to at least one question. Except for a few hours of sleep, she'd been on the computer steadily, doing preliminary research for Tanner. They'd managed to eliminate nearly every guest as a possible suspect and were now down to four men.

When she saw she had e-mail waiting, she clicked on the icon to check who it was from and saw an auto-announce message from her father's company. As soon as she opened it and read the headline, she realized Christopher's money problems were all over.

"They're merging," she called to Tanner, who sat at another computer in the control room. "Christopher and my father. I can't figure out if this is good or bad. They made the announcement as soon as the stock market closed, but the price of Christopher's stock will skyrocket tomorrow. His company is much smaller and less well funded. I know he has options. He can sell them at the peak and make a bunch."

"Twenty million?" Tanner asked.

"Easily. He's had the options for years, so we can't even try to get him on insider trading." She looked at Tanner. "Does this merger make my father safer or put him more at risk?"

"Hilliard would never do anything publicly," he told her. "For the next few weeks, both companies are going to be under a lot of scrutiny."

That made sense. "He'll need my father around to act as the figurehead. Of course. So we've bought some time for him."

Tanner stood and crossed over to her chair. He crouched next to her.

"We don't know that your father was ever at risk. Hilliard isn't killing for the hell of it. He always has a plan."

"I know. It just freaks me out to think that my father trusts him so much. Why can't he see the truth?"

"Maybe he doesn't want to. You've said he likes his world simple."

She nodded. "Seeing Christopher as the bad guy would change everything. There was a time when I spent my whole life wanting to make my father happy. I even took a lot of math and science my first couple of years at college. But he never noticed, not even when I got all A's. In the end, I stopped trying."

"Did you want to go into the family business?" he asked.

"Maybe. I don't know. It wasn't an option. My father continues to believe I'm just like my mother. I helped that along by always saying I didn't have the math gene and pretending to be dumb. It's not a restful way to grow up."

"And with Hilliard feeding him the story about you being weak and crazy, he's not going to believe you're fine."

"Exactly."

"Maybe things can be different now."

"Maybe. I could—" Another e-mail appeared in her in-box. "This could be more news about the merger," she said. "We might get some information from the terms."

She clicked on the mail and was surprised to see it was from Christopher. Instantly she felt cold, as if she'd just stepped into an ice storm. Dread formed a knot in her stomach.

"I know he can't hurt me," she whispered, "so why am I afraid to open the letter?"

"Because he hurt you before and he could be trying to kill you. Being worried is the smart response."

She smiled gratefully. "You do have a way with words."

"Yeah, that's me. A great talker. Want me to open it for you?"

"No. I can handle it." Then she laughed. "After speaking with such bravado, I now want to ask you to stay close in case it tries to bite me."

He stood and grabbed a nearby chair, then pulled it next to hers. "I'm at your service."

She clicked on the e-mail.

Madison, I know you think this is a trick, but your father is very ill. The problem with his heart is getting worse. It's the reason he's finally agreed to the merger. He wants to see it happen before it's too late. You have no idea how much he's worried about you. Your absence is killing him, and I'm not saying that to be dramatic. If you don't believe me, contact his doctor and ask about his recent appointment. Whatever you think about me is fine. I won't go near you until you ask to see me. But you must see your father. You may not have that much time left.

"He's good," Tanner said.

Madison couldn't speak. Her mouth had gone dry and she could barely catch her breath.

"It's n-not true, is it?" she asked in a whisper.

He took her hand. "You know it's not. I have men watching your father around the clock. He hasn't been to a doctor. He's keeping to his normal schedule. He's fine. Hilliard is playing dirty."

She tore her gaze away from the screen and stared at Tanner. "I want to believe you."

"How can I convince you? Do you want me to get a copy of his medical records?"

"Can you do that?"

"Sure. It'll take a day or so, but I can get them."

"Won't that be breaking the law?"

He smiled. "Do you really care about that right now?"

"No."

"Then don't sweat it. I'll get you the records and you can see for yourself that your father is fine." He rubbed her upper arms. "Don't let him get to you, Madison. This is all about winning the game. He's trying to make you blink first."

"I know. It's just that he's doing a really good job. I don't want to worry, but I can't help it. My dad is my only family. He's all I have left. If something were to happen to him…"

"It won't. I promise. I'll get the medical records. What else can I do to set your mind at ease?"

She wanted to ask him to let her see her father for herself but knew that would be a mistake. Leaving the house would put them all in danger. Christopher couldn't be happy that the man he'd hired to find his ex-wife had turned on him. So Tanner's life was also at risk.

She knew that even if she saw her father, she couldn't tell him the truth. The far-fetched story would only confirm his worst fears about her mental state.

"I'm okay," she said. "You've already done so much."

"I can do more."

"No. Really. Get back to work."

She leaned close and kissed him, then pushed him in the general direction of his computer. When he'd moved over, she returned her attention to her screen, but instead of seeing the words and letters, she saw Tanner's face when he offered whatever she needed to help her relax.

He was a good man. Hardly news but still worth noting. She'd never met anyone like him. They were from different worlds, yet they seemed to mesh together well in this one.

What happened after? she wondered. Eventually Christopher would be caught—at least, that was her fantasy. Then what? Would Tanner return to his life and would she return to hers? Would they pretend this had never happened? Would they walk away without any regrets?

She knew she would never forget him, that he had changed her for the better. She was stronger for having known him. He had touched her heart.

Did she want more from him? Even if she did, it hardly mattered. Knowing him as she did, she understood that he would always live in the shadows. A man like him needed a pretty good reason to come out into the light. Was she enough of one?

Chapter 16

Tanner woke to a soft but insistent beeping. It took him a second to place himself, then he realized he'd fallen asleep on the sofa in the control room. Not smart, he thought as he stood and stretched the cramps out of his muscles. He was too tall to fit comfortably on the worn couch and too old to not care about the size of his bed.

But he'd wanted to avoid his bedroom—maybe because lying on the mattress would make him think of Madison, and he hadn't wanted that. He would have been tempted to join her in *her* bed and he knew better than that. After all, this was temporary—there was no point in getting used to anything. So he'd stayed away and now he was stuck with the consequences.

He followed the beeping sound, then grinned. "Hot damn!"

His trusty decoding program had come through. He had access to Hilliard's laptop. Every single file lay at his disposal.

"I love it when a plan comes together," he said.

Before settling down to discover all the gory details about the other man's dealings, Tanner walked into the kitchen and made a pot of coffee. While the water slowly filtered through the grounds, he glanced at the clock. Four-fifteen. It had taken just over forty-eight hours to break the encryption, which meant it had been a damn good program. His record to date had been ten hours.

Coffee in hand, he returned to the control room and set to work downloading all the information. It didn't take him long to figure out Hilliard's filing system. In less than an hour he had a basic timeline of the delivery dates of the jamming-device components and a schedule of payments due and paid. The last one, fifteen million, tied in perfectly with Madison's abduction.

"What are you doing?"

He looked up and saw a very sleepy Madison standing in the doorway. She wore oversize pajamas covered in sheep and cows. Her hair was mussed, her eyes unfocused. God, she was beautiful.

"We got through his encryption," he said, motioning her forward.

"Really? Is it all there?"

"Yeah. Come have a look."

She walked toward him. He pulled her onto his lap and wrapped his arm around her slender waist.

"Here's the payment and delivery schedule for the technology." He clicked on the file.

"Where did he come up with the money?" she asked. "The first payment is twenty million."

"Funny you should ask." He clicked on a few more keys, then pointed. "Interesting sale of company assets."

She peered at the screen. "He sold that building in Tucson and pocketed the proceeds? That can't be legal."

"I'm guessing it isn't. For the second payment, he sold some stock and what looks like a Monet."

Madison groaned, then rested her head on his shoulder. "Not the Monet." She held up her hand. "I know, I know. People can't pay their mortgage and I'm whining about a painting. It's just I loved that piece so much. It was small, of his favorite garden. I wanted it when we got divorced, but Christopher refused. I thought it was because he was being a jerk and keeping it because I loved it. I never thought he would sell it."

"Any idea of what it would bring?"

"A couple million. Have I mentioned I hate him?"

"No, but it was sort of understood."

"And I have lousy taste in men."

"You're making that assumption based on one decision?" he asked.

"It was a really bad decision."

"Fair enough." He kissed her cheek just below the scar. "What woke you up?"

"The smell of coffee. I never could resist it."

He handed her his mug.

"I have the name of his contact," he said, pointing at a line on the screen. "Stanislav. Nothing else. He won't be easy to find."

"Especially with Christopher having access to a ton

of money with the merger. It could be the last payment. If it is, we'll never catch him."

"Don't worry. We'll get him."

"How?"

He scrolled down to the next screen. "I'm still working on that. Between the merger and jamming device, Hilliard is going to be living a pretty high-profile life. We can use that to our advantage. I have a few friends in the federal government. Now that we have Hilliard's computer records, I'm going to make a few phone calls and see what can be done. The U.S. government won't be happy that a defense contractor is buying technology from the Russian Mafia and passing it off as homegrown."

"Sounds like a plan." She handed him back the coffee. "But I still have one question."

"Which is?"

"If Christopher got my father to agree to the merger and he has all the money he needs to buy the rest of the whatever it is, why is he trying to lure me out in the open by telling me my father is sick?"

"You know too much," Tanner told her. "He's afraid of what you'll find out. Plus Blaine probably wants to see you. He can't put off your father forever."

"I guess. Sometimes I think he wants to get to me just to prove he can."

"Does the reason matter?" he asked.

"No. But he scares me. I wish he didn't, but he does."

He didn't like to see fear in her eyes. "I'll keep you safe," he told her.

"For now. But you can't take me on as a full-time job. Eventually I have to return to the real world. Then what?"

"We'll have caught him by then."

"Are you sure? Can you know that?"

He didn't answer her because he couldn't say what she wanted to hear. There were no guarantees in his business—unless it was that death was final. Was that the truth of it? Would Madison never be safe until her ex-husband was dead? If that was the case, was Tanner willing to be the one who pulled the trigger?

Christopher drove into the multilevel parking structure next to the deserted office building. He followed the up arrows to the second level, then headed for the east side of the garage. After parking, he turned off the engine and waited. Less than ten seconds later, another car came up next to his and Stanislav stepped out.

Christopher opened his door and grinned. "I have the money. All of it. Every penny." He'd cashed out his options that morning and collected the proceeds. Sure, it was a lot of money, but it would be worth it. When he announced what his company had created and offered the first demonstration, he would make billions.

"Good. It is important to pay what you owe," Stanislav said. "I'll admit I was worried. When you couldn't get the money before, I wondered if we could do business. I don't like it when people let me down."

Christopher ignored the implied threat in the words. What did he care about all of that now? He had the cash and in return he would get the final components.

There were those who regretted the breakup of the Soviet Union, but he wasn't one of them. Brilliant

Russian minds had created the jamming device, and due to his willingness to deal, he was about to reap the reward.

He walked around to the rear of his car and opened the trunk. A black suitcase lay there.

"Fifteen million," he said.

Stanislav glanced from the bag to him, then called for one of his men. "To count it," he said.

"Sure thing."

While Stanislav's associate counted the cash, Christopher examined the two components Stanislav handed him.

At last, he thought. He would spend the next couple of weeks breaking the parts down and making sure everything worked, then he would announce his "discovery" in a press conference. After that, he would own the world.

He turned the larger piece over, then froze. On the underside was a connector, but nothing was attached. He knew the equipment he'd already bought, and there wasn't anything that would connect to this.

Goddamn son of a bitch. He turned to Stanislav. "It's not all here."

The other man shrugged. "You may be right."

Fury built up inside of Christopher. "You said this was the last payment. You said I would get all the equipment and we would be finished."

Stanislav glared at him. "You said I would receive *my* payment nearly a week ago. This is a business transaction. Time is money. You made me wait, now you pay. Think of it as interest."

Christopher wanted to pull out a gun and start shooting. Fortunately he hadn't brought one with him. Not after the first meeting, where he'd been thoroughly searched. Rage bubbled inside of him. How could this be happening? He needed the damn equipment finished.

"You could, of course, take what you have and figure out the missing piece yourself," Stanislav said with a slight smile. "There is not much to it. Some circuits, a chip or two."

Of course, Christopher thought bitterly. He could have easily figured out the hardware, but microchip design could take months.

"How much?" he asked flatly.

"Not so much. Ten million."

Christopher swore aloud. He didn't have that kind of money. He'd used the last of his options to come up with the cash for this payment and he'd used the bit left over to pay off his gambling debts. He couldn't sell any more shares without making the stock-market watchers nervous and he didn't want that. Blaine had more money than God, but he wouldn't give Christopher a loan without asking a lot of questions.

Ten million dollars. Where could he…

Madison, he thought. She had stock and options worth that much. Maybe more.

"How long do I have?" he asked.

"Another week." Stanislav said. "A generous amount of time."

Perhaps in the world of the Russian Mafia, but it didn't give him all that long to pull his plan together. Fortunately he'd already planted plenty of seeds. Now he just had to make sure he handled things well enough to draw Madison out into the open. Once he had her, the money was his…as was she.

"Thanks, Bill," Tanner said as he leaned back in his chair. "I've already e-mailed you as much as I have."

"This would be easier if you had actual proof," his friend said.

Tanner shifted the phone to his other hand and grinned. "I can't do all your work for you. It would make you feel too guilty about taking your paycheck."

Bill chuckled. "You'd be surprised how much guilt I *wouldn't* feel. I look forward to reading over the material. There's a guy pretty high up in the Russian Mafia working the west coast. I'd love to nail the bastard."

"Then I hope this is the one."

"Me, too. I'll be in touch."

They hung up. Tanner turned to Madison, who paced the length of the room.

"It's done," he told her. "Bill will talk to his team and they'll get going on what they can find out about Christopher's plan to buy the technology. The good news is they're already chasing some guys in the Russian Mafia. We might have given them the information they need to bring them down."

"That would be great. Is Bill in Washington, D.C.?"

"San Francisco." He watched her continue to prowl the room. "Madison, relax. We'll get him."

"But will it be in time? I have this horrible feeling of impending doom. I can't shake it."

"Do your horrible feelings usually come true?"

"I don't know. I haven't had one before."

She stopped in front of the window facing the back-yard and stared out. Afternoon sunlight brought out the pale gold in her blond hair. She wore shorts and a T-shirt, no makeup. She'd been eating regularly since arriving at the safe house and her face had lost its gaunt-ness, but worry took its place.

"Waiting is the hardest part of the job," he told her.

"This isn't a job to me. It's my life." She sighed and faced him. "Sorry. I'm snappy because I'm tense. I need to be doing something, but I'm all caught up on e-mail and I have yet to discover the joys of weekday afternoon television. I guess I could go clean the kitchen."

"Or we could talk."

She smiled. "I must really be getting on your nerves, huh?"

"I like talking to you."

"Okay." She walked to the chair across from his and flopped into the seat. "What do you want to talk about?"

"How about your kids? Tell me about Kristen."

She frowned. "How do you know about her?"

"You had a letter from her in your e-mail file. Some-thing about going to a dance."

"Oh, right." Madison smiled. "She was so thrilled. And transformed." The smile faded. "When I first saw her, she was horribly scarred. She'd been born to teen-age parents who decided to keep her and raise her on their own. One night her dad took her on an errand. It was late and he was in a hurry, so he didn't use a car seat or buckle her in. They were hit by another car and she went flying through the windshield. She was four. Her whole face was lacerated."

"That had to be hard," he said.

"It was worse—her father was kill[...] it was just her and her mom. There was no[...] local doctors did the best they could, but the[...] plastic surgeons. One of her eyelids folded ov[...] the right corner of her mouth pulled down. As she[...] older, her face grew but the scars didn't. Every yea[...] she was more and more misshapen. When I met her, she was fourteen and looked like something out of a horror movie. But she was a sweet kid. Funny and smart. She and her mom had a great relationship. I wanted to wrap them both up and take them home with me."

"Did you?"

The smile returned. "I did one better. I got her help. Two incredibly gifted surgeons worked on her face. They reduced the scar material, got everything back where it was and made her pretty for the first time in her life. She'll always have scars, but the new ones are thin lines easily covered with a bit of makeup."

Madison continued to talk about Kristen's dance experience, but he stopped listening. He would rather lose himself in the pleasure of watching her mouth move when she spoke. He liked how she formed words and used her hands to illustrate a point.

Emotions widened her eyes or brought color to her cheeks. Her mouth curved. Every movement, every action, reminded him how beautiful she was.

But it wasn't just that, he thought. Beauty was easy. It was the woman inside who had him mesmerized. The one who cared about kids she'd never met, who

because she could make
worked hard, that she
sh came to shove, she
t her kids what they

w he couldn't say that
er been intimate with.
f the word.

aid as she folded her
arms over her chest. "I could really take offense at that."

"But you won't."

She sniffed. "What were you thinking about that was more interesting than what I was saying?"

"Not more interesting. Just different. And I was thinking about you. How great you are."

"Oh, please."

"I'm not kidding."

"But I'm not all that special."

"Want to bet?"

She ducked her head and flushed. "Well, thank you."

"You're welcome."

He studied her, knowing that she would not be easily forgotten. That when this was over… "I'll miss you," he said, without meaning to speak the words aloud.

She stared at him. "Tanner?"

"Yeah, yeah, it doesn't mean anything. It's just you're not that bad to have around. I didn't think I'd like you, but I do. You're a hell of a woman. Beautiful, tough, caring."

"I think you're pretty amazing, too."

Which was not a place she should be going, he thought. When this was all over, she would walk away, returning to her regularly scheduled life. He would move on to the next assignment. Neither of them should try to fool themselves into making it something more.

"I'm just the hired help," he said. "Nothing more."

"Actually you're not hired. You won't let me pay you."

"That's because we're sleeping together. Money makes it all too complicated."

She smiled. "A man of principles."

"On my good days."

"What about on your bad days?"

He stood and reached for her hand, then pulled her to her feet. "On my bad days, I'm a hell of a lot of fun."

Then he kissed her.

Madison had made love with Tanner enough times in the past few days to anticipate the pleasure before it even began. All it took was his hand on her waist and his mouth on hers for the melting to begin. She yielded, leaning against him so they could touch everywhere, even as she parted for him and circled her tongue around his.

He tasted of coffee and the oranges they'd had after lunch. Heat began between her thighs and radiated in all directions. Her breasts ached, her muscles tensed and all he'd done was kiss her.

"I can't get enough of you," he breathed against her mouth before breaking the kiss and moving to her jaw.

She echoed the sentiment silently, as she was too caught up in the feel of his lips and tongue on her sensitive skin to do more than gasp her pleasure.

He nibbled on her earlobe, gently biting down on the

flesh before sucking on it. Goose bumps erupted every-where. Her nipples hardened. She wanted him, all of him, right this second. The bedroom was too far away.

Even as the thought formed, she reached for his belt and began to unfasten it. He chuckled against her neck.

"Impatient, are we?"

"Yes. Very."

He grabbed the hem of her T-shirt and pulled it off in one easy movement. Her bra quickly followed, then he turned his attention to her breasts.

He cupped them first, caressing every millimeter of sensitized skin. Then he bent down and licked the very tips of her nipples. Her body clenched in response as she clung to him.

It wasn't enough, she thought, barely able to stay conscious. It would never be enough. She raised her arms. She wanted him naked, but right now she could only experience what he was doing to her.

"More," she gasped, sliding her fingers through his hair to hold his head in place.

He responded instantly, opening his mouth and suck-ing deeply on her breasts. At the same time, he tugged at her shorts. He unfastened the snap and pulled down the zipper. As he licked and sucked and teased her breasts, he slipped his hand inside her panties and be-tween her legs. Then he found that one sensitive spot and began to rub it.

She was already wet and swollen. His clever fingers applied just the right amount of pressure at just the right speed. She tried to part her legs more, but the fabric of her shorts wouldn't let her.

"Tanner!" she gasped as she felt herself getting closer and closer.

He continued to suck on her breasts as he moved his hand between her legs. Tension grew until release became inevitable. She grabbed his shoulders as her body convulsed in perfect bliss. Her release swept through her.

When she was still, he raised his head and began to kiss her mouth. Even as satisfaction rolled through her, desire heated again. She reached for his jeans and finished the job of freeing him from his belt.

"Get naked," he said as he drew back enough to pull off his shirt and toe out of his shoes.

"Right here?" she asked with a grin. "In the control room?"

He pulled a condom out of his jeans pocket, then pushed them and his briefs to the ground. After stepping out of them, he slipped on the protection.

"Does all the high-tech equipment get you hot?"

She laughed as she quickly shed her clothes. "Not especially, but you do."

When she had done as he requested, he lifted her onto his desk and parted her legs.

The height was perfect, she thought as he slipped between her thighs and entered her in one smooth movement. The thick hardness of his erection filled her. She wrapped her legs around his hips and urged him deeper. He obliged her with a slow, deep push.

Nerve endings danced with delight. She reached for him as he reached for her and they met in a kiss that caused their souls to touch. Over and over he filled her, making her stretch and feel and want to scream. Tension grew. He moved faster, the slick friction pushing her closer and closer to the edge until she could only surrender to his will and climax again.

He continued to thrust in and out of her until the last contraction faded. Only then did he give in to his own pleasure and groan out his release.

When they were finished, she felt herself fill with emotions. She wasn't sure what they meant or even what they were. She only knew that she'd never been this close to another person before. She rested her forehead against his and did her best to keep her tone light as she said, "You sure know how to show a girl a good time."

"You're not too bad yourself."

There was more, she thought. More to say, more to experience. Yet something kept her quiet. Maybe it was the realization that nothing about their situation was normal. Danger was supposed to heighten all the senses. Did that explain her attraction to Tanner? And how was she supposed to figure out what was the moment and what was real? It wasn't as if he was going to stick around after the danger had passed. So this was probably all they were ever going to have.

She would make it enough, she told herself, even as she realized she wasn't sure how that was possible.

Madison woke around midnight. Despite a long day and another session of lovemaking, she didn't feel tired. Restlessness stirred her, pulling her from the bed she shared with Tanner.

He slept, unaware of the demons that drove her. She pulled on a robe and walked out of the room.

Once in the kitchen, she searched the refrigerator, but nothing caught her attention. After nibbling on a cookie she didn't really want, she headed for her bedroom, where she could play on her computer. Maybe a couple of card games would still her thoughts.

She'd been cooped up in the house too long, she thought. She needed to get out. There had to be a way she could safely leave. Maybe she and Tanner could discuss it in the morning, she thought as she booted her laptop. The walls were definitely closing in on her.

She moved the cursor to her games program, then decided to check on e-mail first. Only one letter waited for her. She clicked on the icon to open it.

Madison stared at the unfamiliar return address. It took her a second to recognize the last name in combination with her father's company name. His secretary, Alison Harris, had sent the note.

Why on earth would the woman write her? Sure, Alison had worked for her father for fifteen or twenty years, but the older woman had never had much contact with Madison.

She clicked on the mail itself and began to read. Horror chilled her to the bone.

Madison—Please! I'm desperate to get in touch with you. Please call me as soon as you read this. It's your father. He's had a heart attack and he's near death.

Chapter 17

Madison stared at the e-mail for several seconds before panic set it. She scrambled for a piece of paper and a pen, then quickly wrote down the phone number. When she had it, she ran into the control room and picked up the phone.

"Please enter your authorization code."

The computerized voice confused her. She punched in Alison's number, only to hear the instruction again.

"What?" she demanded, then remembered this was Tanner's safe house. The regular rules didn't apply. She hung up the phone.

"I have to know," she murmured as she scanned the room for some way to find out the truth. There were only blinking cursors on various computer screens. How could she—

Tanner's cell phone! She could use that or have him make the call from the regular phone.

She turned toward his bedroom, then froze in place as fear battled with reason. Tanner. He'd said that her father was okay. He'd let her listen to his conversation with one of his men. Her father was fine. He hadn't been going to the doctor. This was just a trick. Christopher was trying to trick her.

"But not through Alison," she whispered to herself.

The gray-haired woman had been with her father for years. Madison had met her countless times. There was no way she worked for Christopher—she'd been employed by Adams Electronics over ten years when Blaine had first met Christopher.

"Why would she lie?"

Nothing made sense. Was it possible that Christopher had been lying about her father being sick, only now he'd had a real heart attack? Stranger things had happened. She had to find out.

She hurried to Tanner's bedroom. He was still sprawled across the bed. She stared at him, not sure if she should wake him or not, then she decided to err on the side of caution. She reached for the cell phone he kept clipped to his jeans and carefully pulled it out of its carrying case. When that was done, she hurried to the far end of the house and punched in Alison's number.

There was a moment of silence followed by the sound of ringing. Thank God Tanner didn't use an access code for his cell.

"Hello?"

Madison's chest tightened. "Alison? Is that you?"

"Madison? Finally. Where are you? I've been trying to reach you for days." The other woman sounded frantic. "Oh, Madison, your father is so sick. He had a heart attack. It's bad. Really bad. He's been having symptoms for days but ignoring them. He was so wrapped up in his work. You know how he is. I made him go see his doctor, who warned him to take it easy, but would he listen?"

Alison began to cry softly. "I'm sorry. It's just I'm the one who found him. He never came out for lunch and I got worried. I went back in his lab, even though he's told me not to. It's his sacred space. He doesn't want anyone mucking around with his experiments." The tears came faster. "He was on the floor. I thought he was dead."

Madison felt tears fill her eyes. How was this possible? "Are you sure? He's really sick?"

"He nearly died. The doctor at the hospital said if I'd found him an hour later, it would have been too late. You have to go see him right away. He's been asking for you."

"I will. What hospital?"

Alison gave her the name and address, along with the direct number for Cardiac Care. Madison wrote it all down. She felt as if she were living underwater where nothing was as it should be.

"I wish he'd listened to his doctor," Alison said sadly.

"When did he go see him?" Madison asked.

"A few days ago. Three, maybe four."

After Madison had listened to Tanner's man give his report. Was it all a lie? Tanner had been so furious about her playing him for a fool, but was the truth the opposite?

"Thanks, Alison," she said. "I'm going to call the hospital right now."

"You do that, honey. I'm praying for him to make it."

"Thank you. For everything."

Madison finished the call and immediately made another.

"Los Angeles General. Cardiac Care."

"Hi. I'm trying to find out about my father. Blaine Adams. I understand he was brought in this afternoon."

"Just a minute."

A couple of seconds later, another woman picked up. "Hi, this is Sandy. Are you Dr. Adams's daughter?"

"Yes. This is Madison."

"Great." The woman sounded intensely relieved. "We've been going crazy trying to find you. Your father was brought in this afternoon in critical condition. The doctors are hopeful he'll pull through, but it's still not a sure thing. The next twenty-four hours will tell. He's pretty out of it, but he's been asking for you."

Madison's tears fell faster now. Oh, God. Her father was really sick. He could die. Christopher had been telling her the truth and she hadn't listened.

"I'll be there," Madison promised. "Please tell him to hold on a little longer. I'll be there."

She hung up the phone and ran to her room. It only took her a couple of minutes to dress. She tucked the cell phone into her jeans pocket, then headed for the cabinet in the control room where Tanner kept the keys to the van. As she reached for them, a faint light from the window glinted on the bracelet.

Damn. The second she walked out of the house, the

alarm would go off. Tanner couldn't possibly sleep through the noise. He would come after her and stop her from seeing her father.

Panic surged through her. She glanced around for the electronic device he'd used to unfasten the bracelet, but she couldn't remember what it looked like. Every second she wasted felt like a lifetime. What if her father died while she was still searching?

Where would it be? Where would—

She saw the medicine cabinet. Drugs, she thought, remembering what Tanner had done to her. It would serve him right, she thought as she ran over and jerked open the door.

Several bottles of liquid and pills sat on shelves. She flipped on a desk light, then began reading the labels. The long names confused her. Besides, she couldn't make him swallow a pill and she didn't know how to use a needle. What if she didn't inject him correctly? What if he wasn't knocked out? She needed a sure thing.

And then she remembered the gun he'd given her. The one with a sedative instead of a bullet.

She returned to the first cabinet, pulled it open and grabbed for the van keys. When they were safely in her other pocket, she searched through the various weapons on shelves until she found the one she recognized. She knew enough to drop the clip and check that there weren't any bullets. She wanted Tanner out of it, not dead.

She ran back to his bedroom. He lay sprawled across the mattress, naked, vulnerable. How could he have done this to her? How could he have lied? She thought about her father, slowly getting sicker and sicker. Fury and pain steadied her arm as she pointed directly at his chest and pulled the trigger.

The shot was quieter than she would have thought. The sedative struck him in the upper left part of his chest, close to his shoulder. His eyes flickered open, then closed. She waited five seconds before shaking him.

"Tanner," she yelled. "Can you hear me?"

He didn't budge.

She dropped the gun onto the floor and ran for the garage.

She was nearly halfway across the cement floor before the computerized voice warned her that she had violated her authorized perimeter. That if she didn't return, an alarm would sound. The shrill siren began as she started the engine. She started to back out before the garage doors had fully opened, and there was an ugly scraping sound, barely audible over the pulsing alarm.

Madison turned on the lights of the van and drove down the street. She had a vague idea of where she was from the trip to Christopher's house a couple of days before. At least she remembered her way to the 110 freeway. Once she was going north on that, she could head west and make her way to the hospital.

Not long now, she told herself over and over again in a litany of prayer. *I'll be there, Daddy. Just hang on for me.*

Tears threatened, but she willed them away. She had to see to drive. There was no point in escaping only to get in an accident. She had to stay strong and in charge. Once she was with her father and he was getting better, she would figure out how to make Tanner pay for what he'd done to her.

* * *

In the hours after midnight even the Los Angeles freeways were empty of traffic. Madison made excellent time to the hospital. She parked in the back, then hurried toward the building. Her heart pounded in time with her steps as she wondered how long it would be until the effects of the sedative wore off. She figured she had at least a couple of hours but not much longer.

She might have taken Tanner's van and his cell phone, but once he woke up, he could still use the land line to call in his team. If only she'd thought to tie him up. That would have bought her more time.

Too late now, she told herself. Once he was awake, he could easily figure out where she'd gone. After all, he had access to her e-mail, which meant he could get to Alison. She would have to warn the other woman.

But first, her father, she thought as she hurried inside and studied the directory.

The large sign told her that Cardiac Care was on the third floor. Madison took the elevator, then followed the arrows to the right department. A woman sat at the front nurses' station.

"I'm Madison Hilliard," she told the nurse. "I'm here to see my father—Blaine Adams. Is he all right? Is he still…"

The nurse, a young woman in her twenties, smiled. "Don't worry, Mrs. Hilliard. Your father is doing all right. Actually, as soon as I told him you were coming, he perked right up."

"He did?"

"Absolutely."

The nurse took her by the arm and led her through the closed double doors into the department. There was a sign saying only family members were allowed for ten minutes every hour. Madison glanced at her watch only to realize she wasn't wearing one.

"Can I stay longer?" she asked. "I haven't seen him in so long."

"Of course. Take as much time as you need." The nurse stopped and pointed at a curtained area. "Just through there."

Madison ran forward and pushed the curtain aside. In that second before the cloth moved, something inside her head screamed out.

But it was too late.

The curtain parted to reveal Christopher sitting in a chair. He had a gun, and when he saw her, he raised it until it pointed at her heart.

"Ah, my lovely wife. Hello, Madison. I'll say this about you—you're consistent."

Her stomach clenched until she was afraid she was going to throw up.

A thousand thoughts filled her mind. Everything from wondering when he'd turned Alison to how he'd managed to get control of some of the hospital staff. There had to be a whole lot on the line for him to go to this much trouble.

The last thing she thought before she inhaled the sweet, sticky smell she remembered so well and everything went black was that Christopher was finally going to win.

* * *

Consciousness returned in the form of a blinding headache. At first, all Madison could focus on was the pulsing pain. She didn't want to open her eyes or move in any way, but she forced herself to turn onto her back and look at her surroundings.

Even with her head throbbing, she saw she was in a small room, on a bed. Muscles ached from the awkward position she'd been in. As she tried to straighten her legs, pins and needles shot through them. She gritted her teeth and moved her feet, then her legs.

The pain made her cry out. Her stomach flopped over, making her nauseous. All she wanted was to curl up and disappear into unconsciousness, but she refused to let herself. She'd gotten herself into this and she had to find a way out.

The ache in her legs faded first. Slow, steady breathing kept her stomach under control. If her previous experience with Christopher knocking her out was anything to go by, the headache was there to stay for at least a few hours. She would simply have to work through it.

She sat up and looked around. The room was maybe ten by ten, with a bed, a sink and toilet and a small window. The quality of light was faint enough to make her think it was dawn. So she'd been out about four hours. There was no sound—not a car driving by, not a dog barking. Wherever she'd been brought, it was in the middle of nowhere.

At least she was alone. Last time, she'd awakened to find herself watched twenty-four hours a day. The constant monitoring had been difficult to take. Better to be alone, she thought as she stood and explored the room.

There was only one door—metal and locked. No food, no change of clothes. In a way it was very much like the room Tanner had taken her to when he'd rescued her. Only a lot more terrifying.

Tanner. She didn't want to think about him, but she had to. How could she have been so stupid as to believe he would turn on her?

It was Christopher, she thought grimly. He'd been smart. Somehow he'd gotten to Alison and had convinced her father's secretary to help him. Madison would have been suspicious of anyone else but not Alison.

Madison drank some water from the faucet and returned to the bed. Tanner would probably have recovered from the sedative, but that wasn't going to be much help to her. Sure, he could trace her to the hospital, but then what? She looked at the bracelet she wore. It only worked within the grounds of his property. No hidden beacon was going to give him a clue. She was on her own.

Christopher was going to kill her. She accepted that. If not today, then soon. The thought of death scared her, but what really made her want to pound her hands against the walls and scream was the thought that Tanner would never know she was sorry to have misjudged him. He would live the rest of his life aware that in the heat of the moment, she hadn't trusted him.

"I was a fool," she whispered into the silence. "I should have remembered Christopher would do anything to get his way. I should have known you were on my side."

Worse, she should have listened to her heart. Over the past couple of days, she'd been feeling things for Tanner. Maybe they were about him rescuing her as much as about the man himself, but they were still there. And they'd made her nervous. She didn't want to be vulnerable to any man. Christopher had taught her the danger of that.

She tried to imagine what Tanner would think when he woke up. He would find her computer and the e-mail. He would start with Alison. But then what? Would the secretary be in hiding? She had a feeling Christopher would take care of that little detail. Which meant Tanner would end up with no way to find her.

It didn't occur to her that he wouldn't look for her. Despite what she'd done, he would come after her. That's the kind of man he was. If only she could tell him how much she regretted what she'd done.

Time passed. When the sun was high in the sky and the small room had become uncomfortably hot, the door opened and Christopher entered.

"I hope you slept well," he said politely as he stood just inside the door.

She stayed on the bed, back against the wall, legs stretched out in front of her, and studied the man she'd been so excited to marry.

He was tall, slim, with dark blond hair and light brown eyes. He was a man born to wear expensive clothes and have them look good. She'd been fooled by a facade of good manners and a great lineage. She'd never seen the real man behind the smile.

When she didn't answer, he sighed. "You're going to make this difficult, aren't you?"

"I'm not inspired to cooperate."

"Even if I threaten to kill you?"

She was proud of herself for not reacting. "You're going to do that anyway."

He smiled. "Probably. But wouldn't you rather it was later?"

"Not if it means having anything to do with you."

Christopher's good humor faded. "We could have been good together, but you had to spoil everything. You couldn't leave well enough alone."

For the first time she realized *he* was the crazy one in the relationship.

"You don't want me," she said quietly. "You've never wanted me. It was always about my father's company."

"Which I have now. Did you hear? There's a merger pending."

She nodded. "What do you want from me?"

"So impatient to be dead?" he asked. "Be careful, Madison. You're only a phone call away from the loony bin."

The thought of being locked away like a crazy person had always terrified her. She did her best to keep the fear small and buried.

He moved over to the bed and sat next to her. "How did you do it?" he asked conversationally. "How did you turn Keane? He's supposed to be the best in the business. You must have told a hell of a story."

His calmness and even temper told her how in control of the situation he thought himself to be. Not comforting for her.

"I told him we were divorced," she said, not seeing any point in keeping the truth from him.

His mouth twisted. "That damn divorce. I hadn't mentioned it to him. That was enough to convince him?"

She shrugged. "It was a start."

"How much does he know?"

Terror swept through her, but this time it wasn't for herself. She'd expected Christopher to come after her, but she didn't want him chasing Tanner.

Christopher leaned close and wrapped his hand around her hair. He tightened his grip until every hair follicle burned.

"You're protecting him?" he asked, sounding incredulous. "Bitch. Did you sleep with him? Was he just as bored with you in bed as I was?"

He released her hair, stood and slapped her across the face. The blow stung, but she refused to react.

"I want you to change your clothes," he said as he walked back to the door. "You'll have to eat, too. No fainting. In fact, nothing out of the ordinary."

She waited, knowing he was finally going to tell her what this was all about. And then, before he could speak, she understood.

"You need more money," she breathed.

"Smart girl. About ten million. We're going to your

broker's office and you're going to sign your stock and options over to me. Just like that."

Before she could respond, he pulled a small electronic device from his suit pocket.

"This is a really interesting piece of work," he said as he flipped up the cover and showed her three buttons. "I invented it when I was in college. A remote control device that can transmit several hundred miles. I tap into satellites with it and send a code to a receiver. Right now that receiver is attached to the brake line of your father's car."

He smiled. "Oh, didn't I tell you? Blaine is driving to San Francisco. It was my idea. You know what the roads are like on the coast route. All those twists and turns. If a car lost its brakes there, the result would be tragic. One push of the button and no more Daddy."

He snapped the cover back in place. "Your call, Madison. Either cooperate or he's dead."

Chapter 18

Madison didn't need any time to think. "I don't care about the money. You can have it all."

Christopher smiled. "Spoken with the easy confidence of someone who has never done without. Not that you should worry. I'll still take care of you." He glanced at his watch. "You'll have a half hour to eat and change your clothes, then we'll drive to the brokerage office and make that transfer. If anything goes wrong—" He waved the remote detonating device.

"Nothing will go wrong," she said quietly.

Fifteen minutes later, she'd forced herself to eat a scrambled egg and some toast. Food was the last thing she wanted, but she agreed with Christopher on the "no fainting" rule. She had no one to blame for her current circumstances except herself. Better to keep up her strength and energy so if an opportunity for escape came, she was ready to take it.

As she sipped on the coffee, she changed out of her jeans into the pale blue suit Christopher had brought her. A white silk blouse and pale gray pumps completed the outfit. She'd just finished brushing her hair then pinning it up in a twist when he reappeared in the doorway.

"Ready?" he asked.

She nodded. "I'm going to need identification," she said. "Even though they know me there, they'll ask for it."

Christopher held out a small purse that matched her shoes. She checked inside and found her wallet, complete with driver's license, along with her passport.

"Did you get these from my place when you kidnapped me or did you take them later?" she asked.

He only smiled. "Let's go," he said, motioning for her to step out of the small room.

Unlike Tanner, Christopher saw no reason to conceal the location of the facility from her. They were in some kind of business complex with rows and rows of small industrial businesses. She glanced around but couldn't figure out what part of town they were in. Still, she did her best to memorize what she could to help the police find the place again. Assuming she ever had the chance to talk to the police.

Christopher put her in the back of a limo, then climbed in himself. With the privacy panel in place, she couldn't see the driver, but he must have already been behind the wheel because as soon as Christopher closed the rear door, the engine started.

"Just so you know I'm not kidding," he said as he began to punch numbers on a cell phone.

She watched him for a second, then realized it was Tanner's phone—the one she'd taken when she'd foolishly escaped.

"Blaine?" he said, speaking into the phone. "How's the drive?"

He listened for a second, then looked at her. "I have a surprise for you. Hold on a second." He passed the phone to her and then removed the remote device from his suit jacket pocket.

She took the phone. "Daddy?"

"Madison!" Her father sounded delighted. "It's good to hear your voice. How are you feeling?"

"Good. I'm feeling really good. How are you?"

"Never better. I'm heading to San Francisco for a conference. Christopher suggested I drive. Fine idea. What a beautiful part of the country. We should all spend a long weekend in Carmel."

Tears burned in her eyes, but she blinked them away. He was fine. He had always been fine. Why hadn't she trusted Tanner? Why had she acted out of fear instead of thinking things through?

"That sounds nice," she said.

"Did Christopher tell you about the merger? Isn't it wonderful news?"

"It's great," she whispered.

"Christopher is taking care of everything. As always. I don't know what I'd do without him around." Her father sighed. "I know you two have had your differences, but I wish you would consider working things out with him. Madison, he's a good man and he loves you very much. He's been distraught these past few weeks, first with the kidnapping, then with you away."

Holding back the tears was nearly an impossible task. If it had been anyone else, she would have wondered how her father could have been so easily fooled. But he was a man devoted to his work. The rest of the world simply faded away. Christopher made his life easier and Blaine appreciated that. For him there was no need to look past the surface.

"I love you, Daddy," she said quietly.

"I love you, too, Madison."

Christopher glared at her, then took back the phone. "We don't want to distract you from your driving for too long, Blaine. Those are tricky roads. You be careful."

She couldn't hear her father's response, but it didn't matter. The warning had been much more for her.

She knew in her heart that Christopher would kill her father without a second thought. No one mattered to him; he just wanted money and power. She was living on borrowed time, as well, but somehow that mattered less. If he killed her this second, she would have only two regrets. First, that she wouldn't be around to help her kids anymore, and second, that Tanner would always believe that she hadn't trusted him or cared for him at all.

The brokerage office claimed five floors in a Century City high-rise. Madison rode the elevator in silence, then stepped out in the elegant foyer and asked for Jonathan Williams.

"I'm sorry," the receptionist told her. "Mr. Williams is on vacation. Did you have an appointment?"

Madison turned to Christopher. "Did you make an appointment?"

He nodded. "Paul Nelson is handling the transaction."

"Then Mr. Nelson," Madison said.

"Of course. I'll tell him you're here." She waited politely for their names.

Christopher put his arm around Madison and squeezed her tightly against him. "Mr. and Mrs. Hilliard."

"Of course." The young woman smiled, then spoke into her headset. "Mr. Nelson will be right out."

In a matter of minutes they'd met the tall, handsome man who would handle the transaction and had been shown into a conference room. Floor-to-ceiling windows offered a view north, toward Hollywood.

"Mrs. Hilliard," Paul Nelson said as he held out a chair. "I understand you want to make some changes in your account."

She took the seat and forced herself to smile at the man. None of this was his fault. It wasn't anyone's but hers. "Yes, please. I wish to transfer some assets into my husband's account."

The broker raised his eyebrows but didn't comment. "Do you have a list of what you would like to transfer?"

She didn't, but Christopher did. He passed over a sheet of paper. Madison didn't bother to look at it. What did the money matter?

"This is just over ten million dollars," Paul said.

"Yes." Madison stared at him as she spoke. She wanted to take the man aside and tell him to get on with it. That her father's life was at stake. Instead she smiled. "I've brought identification with me, if that's the problem."

Paul chuckled. "No, it's not. All right. I'll prepare the withdrawal from your account and the deposit into your husband's account. Mr. Hilliard, will you be putting this into your brokerage account here?"

"Yes."

She noticed Christopher didn't correct the man about their marital status.

Paul left the room, closing the door behind him. Madison rose and crossed to the window.

"What happens after this?" she asked. She knew he wasn't going to let her go.

"We'll get married," he told her. "Something quiet. Maybe we'll fly to Las Vegas. That will seal the merger. In a few months, we can divorce. I'll keep most everything, but I'll leave you enough to live on."

Lies, she thought. Oh, sure, he probably would force her to marry him again, but there wouldn't be a divorce. She knew she would die unexpectedly and that Christopher would play the grieving widower with great style.

She remembered what Tanner had told her about the death of his parents. A car accident. Something about brake failure. How many other people had he killed?

Christopher pulled out the cell phone and punched in a number. When he began speaking, it took her a second to realize it wasn't in English. Russian? she wondered. His Mafia friends? Is that what the ten million was for? The last payment on his jamming device?

As Christopher spoke, the door to the conference room opened. Paul Nelson stepped in.

"Just a couple of quick questions," he said, even as he reached into his jacket pocket and pulled out a gun.

Madison was too stunned to speak. Christopher hadn't turned around, so he didn't see the other three men, all dressed in black, enter after Paul.

She stared in disbelief as her gaze settled on one of them. Tanner!

His dark gaze met hers. She felt him willing her to remain silent. As she had no plans to speak anytime soon, that was easy enough to do. Unfortunately Christopher glanced up and saw Paul holding a gun. He dropped the phone, sprang to his feet and pulled out a weapon of his own. Even as he turned toward the other men, he reached into his jacket pocket.

"No!" Madison screamed. She lunged for him. If he got his hands on the detonator, he would kill her father.

He pulled out the small box and flipped open the cover. Tanner reached him first and savagely kicked his wrist. The box fell to the ground and went skidding across the hardwood floor. She dived for it, even as Christopher grabbed for her. Somewhere behind her a gun chambered a round. A heartbeat later, a bullet exploded just over her head.

Madison ignored the flying plaster. She grabbed for the box and wrapped her fingers around it. Behind her she heard a scuffle as Tanner's men subdued Christopher. She carefully closed the top on the box and breathed a sigh of relief.

Only then did she turn around and watch as Christopher was handcuffed. Paul Nelson slipped his gun back into his holster and patted Tanner on the shoulder.

"Nice work. Good timing."

"Yeah. You, too."

Madison glanced between the two men. "Your friend from the government?" she asked.

Tanner nodded. He crossed to her and crouched next to her. "You okay?"

She nodded and started to stand. He helped her to her feet. She handed him the device.

"It's connected to my dad's car. If you push the button, the brakes go out."

"Do you have your dad's cell number?" he asked.

"Yes."

He fished his phone out of Christopher's pocket and handed it to her. "Call him and tell him to pull over. I'll contact the California Highway Patrol and ask them to pick him up."

Nothing in Tanner's calm expression gave away what he was thinking. It was as if none of this mattered to him. As if she were only a client. But that couldn't be true, she thought. She had to matter.

But first she wanted her father safe.

Fingers trembling, she called him.

"Dad? It's Madison."

"Hello, honey. How are you feeling?"

"I'm fine. Listen to me, Dad, you need to pull over right now. Please. Just pull to the side of the road. There's something wrong with your car."

She waited, breathless, willing him to believe her.

After a long pause, her father said, "Madison, are you taking your medications? It's important that you listen to your doctors. You've been through a lot. We all want you to get better, but you can't rush your treatment."

The unfairness of the situation slammed into her. Why couldn't he just believe her?

"I'm not crazy," she said. "You have to listen to me."

"What's the noise, Madison? Where are you?"

"At my broker's office. Christopher brought me here to have me sign over ten million dollars' worth of shares to him. He needs the money for…" What did it matter? Her father wouldn't listen.

She turned as the men Tanner had brought led Christopher from the room.

"I'll get you, you bitch!" he screamed at Madison. His face turned red and his eyes seemed to bug out. "This is all your fault. I'll get you, and when I do, I'll make you wish you were dead. You hear me?"

The last of her reserves faded. At that moment, Madison couldn't take one more thing. She handed the phone to Tanner.

"My father won't listen to me. Maybe you can make him understand."

Then she grabbed for a chair as her legs gave out and she fainted.

Tanner stood on the tarmac, waiting for the helicopter to land. He had a car ready to take Blaine Adams to his house, where he would finally see his daughter and be questioned by the police.

Hell of a day, Tanner thought. Hilliard had been arrested and there was a warrant out for his Russian friends. Tanner figured the odds of them being found were slim,

Amelia

973

783-300 g

Ribs
Chicken
Fish
Ground beef
buns
Rolls

but the search would send them underground for a while. That might be the best everyone could hope for.

He saw the helicopter in the distance and reminded himself it wasn't a good idea to punch an old man in the face. But that's what he wanted to do to Blaine. Hit him and shake him like a dog for putting his daughter in danger. Tanner believed the old man had acted out of ignorance, but that didn't excuse what had happened. Madison had nearly died because her father couldn't get his head out of his work long enough to take a good look at what was going on around him.

He waited until the helicopter landed, then crossed over to help the only passenger step down.

"Mr. Keane?" Blaine Adams asked when they'd moved away from the helicopter. "I was told you would be meeting me. Perhaps you can explain what's going on. Nothing I've been told makes sense."

"I'm not surprised," Tanner told him. "You know who I am?"

"Of course. You're the man my son-in-law hired to find my daughter after the first company failed. She was kidnapped."

Blaine Adams was in his mid- to late fifties, tall, with white hair and piercing blue eyes. He had the craggy good looks aristocratic men often fall into as they age. He seemed smart enough, but appearances could be deceiving.

Tanner waited until the helicopter had taken off before narrowing his gaze at the old man.

"Christopher Hilliard, who is not married to your daughter anymore, has been arrested on several charges, including kidnapping, extortion, attempted murder and a few other things that haven't been made public. He will most likely be charged with the death of his parents. There was always some suspicion about the way the brakes went out on their car. With the device authorities found attached to the brake line of your car, they may have all the evidence they need."

Blaine paled, then braced himself against the limo. "I don't understand. What are you saying? Christopher would never…"

"Hilliard would do a lot of things, Mr. Adams. He's done them. That technology you're so proud of, the one he worked for months on, was purchased from the Russian Mafia. The only work Hilliard did was that of convincing everyone he invented it. The kidnapping was staged to get you to cough up ransom money. He needed fifteen of the twenty million to make his next installment. The other five million was for his gambling debts."

Blaine shook his head. "No. Not Christopher. He's been like a son to me. Like a brother."

"He's been a lying, cheating son of a bitch who tried to kill your daughter. She's been staying with me, not in some mental home. I've been investigating Hilliard to find out the real story. He tricked her into coming out into the open by convincing her you were dying of a heart attack. She loved you enough to risk her life to see you."

Tanner glared at the old man. "You're a fool and blind where Madison is concerned. I don't know anything about your late wife, but the only thing wrong with Madison's brain is how much she still loves you despite the fact that you turned your back on her. She's not weak or mentally ill. She's tough, determined, intelligent and damn good to have around in a fight. She's a hell of a lot more than you deserve."

"I don't understand," Blaine whispered. "Christopher tried to hurt Madison?"

"Who do you think gave her that scar on her face?"

Blaine stared at him. "She said she fell."

"He pushed her. He also threatened her, kidnapped her and told her if she didn't sign ten million dollars worth of securities over to him that he would blow up the brake line on your car and kill you."

"Oh my God."

Tanner figured the old guy was seconds from passing out. He opened the rear door of the limo and helped Blaine onto the backseat.

"This car will take you home," Tanner told him. "The police and some federal agents are waiting there to question you. Madison's going through that right now. Someone will bring her by later. I suggest you act very, very happy to see her. Whatever you may think about Hilliard being misunderstood or not as bad as everyone thinks, don't you dare say it to her. If I hear you've even *tried* to defend him to her, I'll hunt you down and make you wish you were dead. Do I make myself clear?"

Blaine drew himself up and glared at Tanner. "Mr. Keane, I don't need you telling me how to take care of my daughter."

"Why not? You've been ignoring her and underestimating her for years. Someone has to look out for her."

"I suppose you think that person is you?"

"No one better."

Tanner stepped back and slammed the door shut. When the limo had pulled away, he walked over to his car and prepared to drive back to the safe house. Madison should be finished with her first round of interviews. He'd asked Angel to drop her off there to collect her stuff before she was taken home. Maybe it was stupid, but Tanner wanted to see her one last time. He knew he couldn't say very much, but maybe it would be enough to tell her goodbye.

Chapter 19

Madison finished packing her clothes. She'd already put her laptop in its case and cleared out the bathroom. There wasn't all that much left to do, which meant she had no excuse to linger. But she desperately wanted to see Tanner before she left. Angel had said something about him dropping by, but he hadn't been specific. Madison had a feeling that if she didn't see Tanner now, he would disappear from her life.

She closed the small suitcase and fastened it. Footsteps in the hallway made her tense. She turned, prepared to argue with Angel, but instead saw Tanner standing in the doorway.

Her heart leaped, her chest tightened and deep down in her belly she felt a sensation that could only be relief. He'd come.

Words seemed impossible. She did the only thing that made sense—she ran to him.

He caught her and pulled her hard against him. His arms wrapped around her in an embrace that promised to never let go. She could feel his heat, his strength and his steady heartbeat. His scent surrounded her. At last, she thought with incredible gratitude. Everything could be right with her world.

"I'm sorry," she whispered, still clinging to him. "I'm so sorry."

"Don't be."

He pulled back far enough to stare into her eyes and smile. "I read the e-mail from your father's secretary. The woman has worked for him for years. You've known her since you were a kid. Why wouldn't you trust her?"

"I should have known Christopher could get to anyone. It's just, between talking to her and then speaking with someone at the hospital—it all sounded so real."

"I know. Hilliard had a lot on the line and he was playing for his life. He would have done anything to get you out in the open. Don't blame yourself."

"Who else is there?" she asked. "Are you okay? Did the sedative hurt you?"

"It gave me a hell of a headache, but I've recovered."

She studied his face, the strong lines, the dark eyes, the mouth that could take her to paradise.

"How did you find me?" she asked. "I knew you could trace me to the hospital, but after that…"

He touched her chin, then tucked her hair behind her ears. "My cell phone. It has a tracking device in it."

Of course. "I'm glad, because I was really scared. I

knew this only worked in the house." She held out the bracelet she still wore.

"We should take care of that." Tanner led her to the control room, where he quickly removed the metal band.

"Better?" he asked.

"I guess."

They weren't touching now and she missed the contact. She missed him. The last few hours had been crazy. But she didn't know what to say to him.

"Tanner, I—"

He pressed his fingers to her mouth. "Don't say anything, Madison. You don't have to."

"Yes, I do. You saved me. Not just from my ex-husband but in a hundred other ways. I lost faith, and you gave that back to me. You showed me I was tough and capable."

"You always knew that."

"Maybe, but I never had to prove it before." She shrugged. "I shot you."

"Good for you. You did what you had to in order to survive."

"Oh, right. I ran straight to the enemy."

"You didn't know that. The point is you needed to escape from me and you did."

His casual acceptance of her actions made her heartsick. "I should have trusted you."

"We've been over that." He leaned close and kissed her forehead. "The reality of all this is you've known me ten days. In a dangerous situation, everything is heightened. Senses, reality, feelings. But in time you go back to your regular life and you reevaluate what hap-

pened. You have a lot to be proud of. You were tough
from start to finish. You never gave up. Hold on to that."

"Nice words," she said as her stomach tensed. "It
sounds a lot like a goodbye speech."

"It is."

Pain slammed into her. "But you can't. We've been
through so much. It has to mean something." *I have to
mean something.* But she couldn't bring herself to say that.

"Of course it does," he told her. "You're amazing and
I'll never forget you."

"But?"

"But this isn't real. You're reacting to the danger."

Great. Now he was telling her she didn't know her
own heart? "What? You're saying this is like the Stock-
holm syndrome? That I've fallen for you because of
what we've been through?"

He nodded. "I know that seems cruel, but in time
you'll see that I'm right. You need to get back to your
own life. See your friends, get back to work, establish
a routine. I'm not saying you'll forget me completely,
but in six months, I won't matter the same way. If we
were to start something now, you'd quickly regret it, but
you'd feel too guilty to tell me."

"You're wrong," she said. "You're completely
wrong."

"You can't know how much I want to be. I've seen
it happen."

"I'm not her. You're not him."

"We might as well be."

As he spoke, she saw the pain flash through his eyes.
She reacted instinctively, reaching out for him. He hes-

itated at first, then he gathered her close and pressed his mouth to hers.

It was a kiss of desperation, of one last time before they were apart forever. She clung to him, hoping to convince him with her mouth and her body that this was the most real relationship she'd ever been in. She strained to get closer, to crawl inside of him. Tears spilled from her eyes.

"I love you," she whispered when he drew back. "Why can't you believe me?"

"Don't cry," he said, brushing her cheeks with his thumbs. "I'm not worth it."

"Of course you are."

He lingered against her scar. "I want you to think about why you're keeping this," he said as he stared into her eyes. "If it's for you, if it makes you feel strong and empowered, then don't change anything. But if you keep it for any other reason, then maybe it's time to put it behind you. Don't let Christopher define your future."

She couldn't stop crying. Sobs built up in her chest, although she refused to give in to them.

"Did you hear me?" she demanded. "I love you."

He bent down and kissed her. "You have touched me in ways I would never have thought possible."

Damn the man. He wasn't even going to acknowledge her feelings. "What happens if I feel the same way in six months?" she asked.

"You won't."

"But if I do?"

"Goodbye, Madison."

"Tanner! No!"

The sobs claimed her and she couldn't speak. She had the sense of being alone, so very alone. Then someone was with her, but the arm that offered support wasn't familiar, and when she was finally able to see, the eyes that watched her were pale and empty.

"He's gone," Angel told her.

She nodded and tried to pull herself together. She still had to face her father and help him make sense of all that had happened. She still had a life.

But she didn't want any of it. Not without Tanner.

"Is it because I didn't trust him?" she asked.

Angel shook his head. "No. He understands that. Any of us would have reacted the same."

"Then why?"

"It's like going on vacation. You want to stay in your beachfront bungalow forever, but it's not real life. At some point you have to get back on the plane and go home."

"Tanner is my home, but he won't believe that."

Angel stared at her for a long time. Finally he reached into his jeans back pocket and pulled out a business card. There was nothing on it but a phone number.

"Six months," he said. "If you still feel the same way about him, then you call this number."

Six months. It felt like a lifetime, but having a way to get in touch with Tanner gave her hope.

"You'll see," she said.

Angel didn't look convinced. "Maybe. Now come on, dollface. Let's get you home."

Madison slept for nearly twenty-four hours. When she awoke, she was in the bedroom where she'd grown up, surrounded by stuffed animals and school awards.

It was early evening, still light, and she had the sense of having gone so far, she might never find her way back.

After showering and dressing, she made her way downstairs. The house was familiar. Memories lurked at every corner. Some pleasant, some less so. The ghost of her mother was not to be found. The woman had never really lived here in life, so why would she linger in death?

Madison found her father in his study. But instead of sitting behind his desk, engrossed in papers, he sat in a leather club chair, a drink in his hand. When he saw her, he put down the glass, stood and walked over.

"Madison," he said before pulling her into his arms and hugging her.

She couldn't remember the last time they'd embraced. He might have hugged her at her wedding but not since. Once things had started to go wrong in her marriage, he'd disappeared behind disapproval and lectures.

"I'm so sorry," he told her, echoing what she'd said to Tanner. "I spent most of last night with the police and federal agents, then had another round with them this morning. The things they told me. The things Christopher did."

He stepped back and studied her, then rubbed his thumb against the scar on her cheek. "My beautiful baby girl. What has he done to you?"

She covered her hand with his. "Not so much as you'd think."

"But how he treated you. The things he did. I can't believe he had you kidnapped. Yet it's all true. He's in jail, you know. As are a few people who worked for him. And Alison. He got to her years ago. She has a son with a drug problem. Christopher paid for his rehabilitation, and when that didn't work and he was back on the streets, Christopher made sure he was safe. She was afraid if she ever came to me with the truth that her son would be killed."

Madison led the way to the sofa and sat next to her father. "It's a lot to take in."

"Too much. He fooled us all." His mouth twisted. "No. He didn't fool you, did he? You tried to tell me and I wouldn't listen. I nearly got you killed."

"When we were first married, I believed in him, too," she said. "It was only after that I realized there was something wrong."

Her father pulled her close. "To think he wanted to lock you away and I would have let him. I'll never forgive myself for that."

"You were busy with your work."

Her father grimaced. "How right you are. I have a body of work to be proud of and I nearly lost my only child. I've been doing a lot of soul-searching, Madison, and I don't like what I've learned about myself. I've been self-centered and have taken the easy way out. That's what it was all about with Christopher. It was so much easier to let him be in charge. To let him make the decisions. Then I could spend time in my precious laboratory. But at what price?"

She appreciated the words and the hug. Although they couldn't go back and change time, maybe they could start over.

"At least there's time to stop the merger," Blaine said. "I can't believe I let him talk me into that." He sighed. "No. I encouraged it. Again because it would make my life easier. I'm going to have to spend less time in the lab and more time in the real world." He smiled down at her. "I don't suppose I can convince you to come be part of the company."

"I don't know," she said honestly, stunned he would even consider it. "I have my work with my kids."

He frowned. "What kids? Oh, the charity work. The surgeries. I don't know anything about that. I'm sorry, Madison. I don't know a lot of things. Can you ever forgive me?"

"Of course."

He put his arm around her. "I want to hear everything about your work. If you wouldn't mind, would you start at the beginning and bring this foolish man up to date on your life?"

"I'd be happy to." Then, in a move that shocked her and most likely shocked him, she began to cry.

"What's wrong?"

"Nothing. Everything. I'm so confused and Tanner just left me. He said that I don't know what I feel about him. That I'm just reacting to the danger. But I don't think that's true. I think I love him very much."

Her father smiled at her. "I am probably the worst person to bring this problem to. I know nothing about relationships. Not even friendships. The past two days have more than proved that."

"I know."

"But I would very much like to listen."

She leaned against his shoulder and sighed. "Then I'll tell you."

Chapter 20

Two weeks after Tanner left

Madison gripped the phone. "Angel, you're not cooperating."

"I know, dollface. Cooperation isn't in my job description. I gave you the phone number so if you still want to talk to him in six months, you can find him. That's it. By my watch, we're talking fourteen days. Go. Live your life."

She gritted her teeth in impatience. "Will you tell him I called."

"Probably not."

"You're the most infuriating man."

"So I've heard. Anything else?"

"Christopher's dead."

"Yeah. We got that news flash, too. Inside job. Killed in his cell in jail. We figure it was his friends in the Mafia. They didn't like him making things messy. So you're free of him. That's good."

"I know. I can even feel sorry for him—now that he can't threaten me anymore."

"You're more generous than he deserves. I'm hanging up now."

"Angel, wait. Tell him…tell him I miss him."

"Not a chance."

He disconnected the phone.

Madison replaced the receiver and stared out of her new office window. She'd accepted a job as a director at Adams Electronics while continuing to work a couple of afternoons a week at her charity. She wanted to keep in touch with the children she'd already helped, but she couldn't turn down the chance to work with her father. Not after all the time they'd lost.

Slowly her life had returned to normal. The only thing missing was Tanner. She ached for him. Five months and two weeks, she told herself. Time would pass and then he would have to believe her.

Five weeks after Tanner left

"Angel, I have to talk to him."

"Tell me why."

"I can't."

"You won't," the man said. "Are you sick?"

"No."

"Dying?"

She glanced at the plastic stick in front of her—the one clearly indicating she was pregnant—and grinned. "Never more healthy in my life. That's not the point."

"That's exactly the point. Give it up, Madison."

"I can't. I love him. You really have to have him get in touch with me. This is important. Seriously, life-changing important."

"Which means what?"

She leaned back in her sofa. "That you should get him to come see me. I mean it, Angel. When he finds out what I have to tell him, he'll be really grateful."

"Like I believe that. The answer is no. Stop calling me. Every week we go through this and every week I tell you it's not gonna happen."

She was too happy to be angry with Angel or frustrated by Tanner's stubbornness. She was having his baby. A child of their own.

"We have a tradition now," she said. "When Tanner finally comes to his senses, you're going to miss me."

"Sure. Like lice. Listen, dollface—"

"Angel, it's a new century. You have to stop calling women 'dollface.'"

"It's my trademark."

"It's annoying."

"Good. Now are you going to leave me alone?"

"Nope. He matters too much. I'll phone you next week."

"If it's important to you."

"It is. Oh, Angel? Do you tell him I call?"

She asked the question every week and every week he'd told her no. This time he paused.

"Sometimes."

"Does he say anything?" she asked cautiously.

"No, Madison. He doesn't say anything."

Three months and one week after Tanner left

The good news was the morning sickness had pretty much faded and Madison had actual cleavage for the first time in her life. The even better news was that she and the baby were perfectly healthy and growing just as they should.

The bad news was she missed Tanner with a desperation that only deepened with each passing day.

It was nearly nine when she picked up the portable phone to make her weekly call to Angel. She'd gotten in the habit of calling him at night, so that when they finished she could curl up in bed and pretend Tanner had heard every word. That he cared about her and that it was killing him to be so far away from her.

At what point did she let go? she wondered. Tanner had been concerned that her feelings weren't real, that they were only about circumstances. How could she prove otherwise to a man who refused to speak with her or see her? Was he really trying to give her the space he thought she needed or did he not care about her? Was her love one-sided?

Six months, she told herself. She would give him the six months he'd offered her. On that date, she would call for the last time. She would also tell Angel about the baby. She had hoped to tell Tanner herself, but if he refused to talk to her, there was little she could do.

"But that's nearly three months away," she told herself as she dialed the now-familiar number.

Angel picked up on the second ring. "You're consistent," he said by way of greeting. "I'll give you that."

"Thank you."

"Feeling okay?"

"I'm fine. Eating, sleeping, all the usual bodily functions."

"Good."

She was also finally showing. Her tummy was round, her body lush…or almost lush. How she wanted to share this with Tanner. She wanted him to be a part of her life, of their child's life. But if he didn't want that…

"Is he being stubborn or does he really not care?" she asked.

"Dammit, Madison."

"I want to know. This is hard for me, Angel. I miss him. My feelings aren't going away. You and I both know that—why can't he?"

"You know the rules," he reminded her.

"Screw the rules. I love him. If he were here right now, I'd tell him that. I'd tell him that I miss him in my life. That he's the best man I've ever known."

"He'd tell you you need to get out more."

"Maybe." She smiled. "How are you?"

"What?"

"We always talk about me and Tanner. What's going on with you? Are you seeing anyone?"

"I'm not talking about my personal life with you."

"Why not? I'm a good listener and I can give you the female perspective."

"I don't need it."

"Always the tough guy," she teased. "Come on. Who is she? A model? I can see you with a model. Or maybe a schoolteacher. A single mom?"

He growled, which made her laugh.

"Come on, Angel. Humor me. We have another three months to go."

"You're really going to hang on that long?"

"Yes. After six months I'll stop calling, but I won't stop loving him."

"Swear?"

She heard the word, but it hadn't come from the telephone. Instead the sound had come from the doorway of her bedroom.

Madison let the phone drop onto the comforter as she turned and saw Tanner standing in the darkness. She couldn't see the details of his features, but she recognized him.

Too stunned to speak, she could only watch as he crossed to the bed and picked up the phone. He turned it off before tossing it back on the mattress, then crouching in front of her.

"Are you sure?" he asked, his voice low and thick.

The light from her nightstand illuminated his features. He was gaunt, with circles under his eyes. He looked as if he'd been to hell and lived to tell the tale.

"What happened?" she asked as she touched his cheek. "Were you sick?"

"I missed you. I took every dangerous assignment I could and still I couldn't forget you. You're a part of me—under my skin, in my bones. I breathe you." He took her hand in his and squeezed her fingers. "Madison, are you telling the truth? Do you really love me? Because if you don't, I can't make it. You're my world. This is killing me."

She leaned forward and pulled him close. Then he was on the bed and they were kissing as if they had a lifetime to make up for.

"Of course I love you," she whispered as she pressed her mouth against his lips, his cheeks, his chin. "I've been calling every week, trying to tell you."

"I know. Angel taped the calls and forwarded them to me. I couldn't stand listening to them and I couldn't stop playing them over and over. I needed it all to be true, even as I told myself it couldn't be."

"Stubborn man," she said contentedly. "Do you believe me now?"

"I have to. I need to be with you." He touched her face. "You got rid of the scar."

"It seemed the right thing to do. There's still a faint mark, but I don't need the reminder anymore."

He stared into her eyes. "I love you, Madison. I don't deserve you and you can do a hell of a lot better than me, but I still love you. Marry me. I'll spend the rest of my life taking care of you. I love you with every part of myself. For always."

The happiness filling her was as tangible as the blood in her body. "How do you feel about children?" she asked.

He blinked at her. "I like kids. I want to have kids with you."

"Good."

She took his hand and slid it under the thick comforter to her stomach. He moved over the roundness of her belly, then stared at her.

"You're pregnant?"

She nodded. "I wanted to tell you before, but you weren't taking my calls."

He swore under his breath. "That's what you had to tell me a few weeks ago. The thing you said was important."

"Exactly. I didn't want to have that first emotional exchange with Angel. I mean I like the guy and all, but he's not my type. I seem to be a one-man woman. You're stuck with me, big guy. Guess you're going to have to get used to it."

Tanner didn't know what combination of events had brought him to this moment or why Madison cared about him. But here he was with her, with a baby on the way and a future filled with promise.

He began to laugh. She joined in and they clung to each other.

"I'm happy about the baby," he said.

She grinned. "I got that. I'm happy, too. Now we just need a dog."

"And a house."

"Good idea," she said.

"I need a less dangerous job."

"I agree."

He kissed her, then smiled. "I proposed."

"Yes, you did."

"You didn't answer."

"Oh. Sorry. I meant to." She pulled him close. "Yes, I'll marry you. I want to spend the rest of my life with you."

"Living happily ever after."

"Do you think that's likely?"

He stared into her eyes and saw all the happy days ahead. "Absolutely."

* * * * *

SAGA

National bestselling author

Debra Webb

A decades-old secret threatens to bring
down Chicago's elite Colby Agency in
this brand-new, longer-length novel.

COLBY
CONSPIRACY

While working to uncover the truth behind
a murder linked to the agency, Daniel Marks
and Emily Hastings find themselves trapped
by the dangers of desire—knowing every
move they make could be their last....

Available in October,
wherever books
are sold.

Where love comes alive™

eHARLEQUIN.com

The Ultimate Destination for Women's Fiction

For **FREE online reading,** visit
www.eHarlequin.com now and enjoy:

Online Reads
Read **Daily** and **Weekly** chapters from
our Internet-exclusive stories by your
favorite authors.

Interactive Novels
Cast your vote to help decide how these
stories unfold...then stay tuned!

Quick Reads
For shorter romantic reads, try our
collection of Poems, Toasts, & More!

Online Read Library
Miss one of our online reads?
Come here to catch up!

Reading Groups
Discuss, share and rave with other
community members!

For great reading online,
visit www.eHarlequin.com today!

If you enjoyed what you just read,
then we've got an offer you can't resist!

Take 2 bestselling love stories FREE!

Plus get a FREE surprise gift!

Clip this page and mail it to **Silhouette Reader Service™**

IN U.S.A.	**IN CANADA**
3010 Walden Ave.	P.O. Box 609
P.O. Box 1867	Fort Erie, Ontario
Buffalo, N.Y. 14240-1867	L2A 5X3

YES! Please send me 2 free Silhouette Intimate Moments® novels and my free surprise gift. After receiving them, if I don't wish to receive anymore, I can return the shipping statement marked cancel. If I don't cancel, I will receive 4 brand-new novels every month, before they're available in stores! In the U.S.A., bill me at the bargain price of $4.24 plus 25¢ shipping and handling per book and applicable sales tax, if any*. In Canada, bill me at the bargain price of $4.99 plus 25¢ shipping and handling per book and applicable taxes**. That's the complete price and a savings of at least 10% off the cover prices—what a great deal! I understand that accepting the 2 free books and gift places me under no obligation ever to buy any books. I can always return a shipment and cancel at any time. Even if I never buy another book from Silhouette, the 2 free books and gift are mine to keep forever.

240 SDN D7ZD
340 SDN D7ZP

Name	(PLEASE PRINT)	
Address	Apt.#	
City	State/Prov.	Zip/Postal Code

Not valid to current Silhouette Intimate Moments® subscribers.

Want to try two free books from another series?
Call 1-800-873-8635 or visit www.morefreebooks.com.

* Terms and prices subject to change without notice. Sales tax applicable in N.Y.
** Canadian residents will be charged applicable provincial taxes and GST.
All orders subject to approval. Offer limited to one per household.
® and ™ are trademarks owned and used by the trademark owner and/or its licensee.

INMOM05   ©2005 Harlequin Enterprises Limited

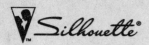

COMING NEXT MONTH

SIMCNM0905